SARANORMAL

Kindred Spirits

WITHDRAWN

by Phoebe Rivers

SIMON SPOTLIGHT

New York London Toronto Sydney New Delhi

SIMON SPOTLIGHT
An imprint of Simon & Schuster Children's Publishing Division
1230 Avenue of the Americas, New York, New York 10020
Copyright © 2013 by Simon & Schuster, Inc.
All rights reserved, including the right of reproduction in whole or in part in any form.
SIMON SPOTLIGHT and colophon are registered trademarks of Simon & Schuster, Inc.
Text by Heather Alexander
For information about special discounts for bulk purchases, please contact Simon & Schuster Special Sales at 1-866-506-1949 or business@simonandschuster.com.
Manufactured in the United States of America 0513 OFF
First Edition 10 9 8 7 6 5 4 3 2 1
ISBN 978-1-4424-6852-8 (pbk)
ISBN 978-1-4424-6853-5 (hc)
ISBN 978-1-4424-6854-2 (eBook)
This book is is cataloged with the Library of Congress.

Chapter 1

"Suddenly the curtain moved all by itself."

The late June sun found its way onto the front porch. I squinted into the glare at my best friend. "How?"

Lily Randazzo shrugged. "No one was standing anywhere near the window. And it was closed, so it wasn't a breeze that moved it."

Lily's voice grew quiet. "Everyone in room seventeen of the Spalding Inn sensed what was happening. Mr. Spalding was there, in that very room, pushing back the curtain and looking out the window. He was staring at the pond where he had drowned fifty years ago."

"Drowned?" I repeated. "Wait, is Mr. Spalding . . . dead?"

"He's d-d-dead?" Lily's five-year-old sister, Cammie, stuttered.

"Totally dead," Lily confirmed. "Now he's a ghost trapped in the inn."

"Ghosts are scary." Cammie tugged their dog, Buddy, closer.

"Even scarier," Lily continued, "was when Mr. Spalding's ghost pulled down the window shade. Right after he did that, there was this supercreepy wailing noise that sounded like it was coming from within the walls and from under the floors. Everyone was so freaked out. . . ."

"What was it?" Cammie asked. The color drained from her normally rosy cheeks.

"The ghost of Mr. Spalding was crying out in pain and frustration!" Lily explained, as if it were the most natural thing in the world.

"Did you help him?" Cammie grasped Buddy tightly.

Lily gently tugged one of her sister's black braids. "No, silly. I wasn't there. I was watching a movie."

"What movie?" I asked.

"*The Haunting at the Spalding Inn*. It was soooo good! And Justin Drexler was totally amazing! He played Mr. Spalding's great-grandson. At the end of the movie, you find out . . . oh, I don't want to ruin it for you!"

"No, tell me!" I said. "You know scary movies and I don't mix. I'll never see it."

"Well, you find out that Justin's character is a ghost too! I had no idea the whole time . . . he's such a great actor, Sar! I think he might get nominated for an Oscar for his performance."

Justin Drexler was the guy Lily—and half my friends, to be honest—had a crush on. He was a pop star turned movie star.

"And look at how amazing-looking he is! He's even cuter with this new haircut!" Lily extended her phone to me. On the screen I could see a picture of a smiling guy with brown hair. He was definitely cute. Lily continued to gush. "And he has this great blog where he talks about all sorts of stuff, like what charities are important to him. I also read on his blog that he's writing a book! He's really into talking about how anyone can do anything they put their minds to. He's so positive! I can't wait for his book to come out!"

"Really?" Reading wasn't Lily's thing. I could finish an entire book in the time it took her to daydream through the first page.

"I know, right?" Lily grinned.

Lily continued to talk about Justin, and I did my best to listen, but I was a little preoccupied. My mind was on another guy. I tried to change the subject and hoped I wasn't being too obvious.

"So, Buddy's previous owners are coming for a visit soon, right?" I asked as I reached over to rub Buddy's belly. "When is that? And is that kid coming with them this time?"

"Who?"

Him. The boy with the white-blond hair. The boy with the piercing green eyes. The boy I couldn't stop thinking about.

"The grandkid. What's his name . . . Mason?" I asked. Of course I knew his name. I'd tattooed it on my brain ever since I saw his photo. Lily was forever crushing on celebrities like Justin Drexler, but I was crushing on a boy who wasn't famous. A boy I'd only seen in one picture.

"It's Mason," Lily confirmed. "Mason has a little brother and sister who are twins. I think they're nine. They're supposed to visit sometime this week."

I nodded, not wanting to press for any more details but hoping she would offer more. She didn't. Lily looked back down at her phone, checking out a few more pictures of Justin before putting it down with a happy little sigh. Her eyes wandered over to the small sign that advertised Lady Azura's business: PSYCHIC, HEALER, MYSTIC.

"I bet Lady Azura would really like *The Haunting at the Spalding Inn*. She would definitely appreciate Justin's convincing portrayal of a ghost. You should totally take her to see it, Sar! It's not *that* scary!"

I gazed at the large bay window. The heavy red curtains blocked my view into her fortune-telling room. The curtains had been closed all the time lately. "She's too busy with nonstop clients these days to go to the movies," I replied.

"I think it's so cool," Lily gushed. "I mean, before everyone realized that she could communicate with the dead, no one knew about Stellamar. We were just this quaint New Jersey shore town. Now Stellamar is famous! Lady Azura is famous! Can you imagine how fun it must be to have powers like hers?"

I poked my finger through a small hole in the hem of my T-shirt. Could I imagine what it was like? Yeah, I pretty much could. "It's not all fun all the time," I replied slowly. "I mean, some of her clients are . . . well, complicated. It can be really stressful sometimes."

"But she has these amazing abilities. And she's famous! Reporters come here!"

"They're gone now," I pointed out. Right after Lady Azura had uncovered the Meyers' jewels, the story went viral, and reporters camped out on our porch for a couple of weeks. Once I even had to sneak out the back door to get to school.

Lily folded the green paper into a fan. "I liked having them here. Why did they all leave so suddenly?"

I smiled. Lily used to dance down the sidewalk to our house. She jetéd and twirled for the reporters. She hoped one of them would discover her and bring her to Hollywood. Never happened. They were only interested in Lady Azura and her powers, and soon even she wasn't all that interesting anymore.

"Kiwi, the Australian teen pop star, was trampled by a horse at a ranch in Montana. They all left yesterday to cover that story," I explained.

"That stinks. Is Kiwi okay?"

"Bruised her toes. Vocal cords are fine." I watched a frazzled-looking woman with long, wildly curly hair shuffle slowly across the street toward our house. She titled her head to better read the number hanging beside the front door. *Client*, I thought. Another client coming to call.

I hated that I felt jealous. All year I had been trying to help Lady Azura grow her fortune-telling business. I'd made flyers and posted online messages. Now, *boom!* After the Meyers' case made headlines, everyone wanted to see Lady Azura.

It's a good thing, I told myself. *I should be happy for her.*

Lily sang Kiwi's latest song, "Dancing Down Under," while performing a series of wiggles and kicks that went with the song. Cammie tried to mimic the steps. I sat on the porch floor, watching an elderly man and woman head toward our house. The woman held a heavy-looking pocketbook in one hand and grasped the man's arm with the other. He had a slight limp. More clients.

"Sara, it's easy. Try it," Lily called.

I didn't move. Instead I tracked three more people trailing the elderly couple to the house. A man with wire-rimmed glasses. A man in a bathing suit with bits of seaweed clumped in his wet hair. A woman in spandex shorts and a jogging top, covered with dirt. She had a large gash on her left leg that oozed blood. I wondered what had happened.

Buddy barked. A high-pitched yelp, repeated again and again.

"Shh!" Lily said, interrupting Kiwi's song.

Buddy pricked his ears and turned his head toward the street. Toward the line of people forming behind the frazzled-looking woman with the crazy hair.

I sighed. I'd planned on spending time with Lady Azura before Dad got home from work. That was never going to happen with all these new clients waiting to see her.

Buddy continued to bark.

Lily stopped singing. "What do you see, Buddy? Do you see a squirrel?" She scanned the front yard.

"There's no squirrel," I said. "It's all those people. Buddy's upset by all those people."

Lily scrunched her nose, already spattered with early-summer freckles. "People?"

I waved to the growing line. "Them."

Lily seemed confused. "What people? Sara, there's just one woman standing by the curb."

"She has a lot of hair," Cammie whispered to me.

I took another look. A closer look. My stomach clenched. My left foot did that weird tingly thing. Lily was right. There was just one woman. One alive woman. But there were other people too. Other people only I could see.

All the other people were dead.

Ghosts.

I bit my lip. I can see ghosts. I can talk to them too. If Justin Drexler was really a ghost, I'd probably have a much easier time meeting him. I was born with this ability, and other ones too. But I don't really like to talk about it.

Not even with my best friend.

I could tell her now, I realized. I'd been thinking about telling Lily for months. I was sure she wouldn't judge me for it. Maybe she'd even think it was cool. At least, I liked to think that maybe she would. After all, she liked ghost movies so much . . . maybe she'd like knowing that her best friend was living a real life ghost movie.

It felt wrong to keep such a big secret from her. Lily thought she knew everything about me: that I moved from California last summer, that my mom died when

I was born, that I'm good at art, that I get hiccups when I laugh too hard. What she doesn't know is what really makes me "me."

My big secret.

"Oh, I know that." I forced a laugh. "I was exaggerating. It just seems like Lady Azura has a never-ending line of people outside. That's all."

I couldn't do it. Not now. Not in front of Cammie, who totally couldn't keep a secret. Not when summer was just beginning. . . . Seeing ghosts isn't like confessing being scared of the dark or sleeping with a teddy bear.

The front door squeaked open. A tall woman I didn't know stepped into the sunlight.

She smiled at us. Her eyes were red and puffy from crying. Then she lowered her head and hurried toward the silver car parked at the curb.

Lady Azura's tiny body looked childlike framed in the doorway. A few stray pieces of her long, mahogany-dyed hair skimmed her false eyelashes. She smiled, and I could see she'd applied a fresh coat of crimson lipstick. I could also see the exhaustion tugging at her papery skin. All these clients wanted her to reach out to the dead for them. They all wanted something from her. I felt bad for her. Calling up ghosts took a lot of energy.

"Lady Azura, have you heard about the new movie *The Haunting at*—"

"Later, Lily dear. Sorry." Lady Azura beckoned to the woman with the hair. "Mrs. Merberg, please come in. I am so sorry I am running late."

Mrs. Merberg slowly climbed the porch stairs and shuffled through the door. Her shoulders slumped, as if she dragged a fifty-pound weight on her back.

Then I watched the elderly man and woman enter my house.

And the man with the glasses.

And the guy in the wet bathing suit.

And the jogging woman with the nasty gash.

One by one, each spirit entered my house.

Lady Azura gave a little wave, then shut the door behind her.

Behind *them*.

My stomach churned with dread.

My house was filled with ghosts.

Chapter 2

"Spices. We need to spice things up," Dad declared.

I peered into the pantry. "What kinds?"

"Oregano, red pepper, black pepper, basil, and parsley." Dad plunged his hands into a mixture of ground beef and bread crumbs. He'd changed from his button-down work shirt into a worn T-shirt that said CALIFORNIA AVOCADO FESTIVAL.

"It seems like a long time ago, doesn't it?" I pointed to his shirt. My aunt Charlotte lives on an avocado farm, and we used to go to the festival every year. She was always trying for a blue-ribbon avocado. The best she ever got was third, which I guess is okay when it comes to pitted fruit.

Dad glanced down. "It does. In a good way, right?"

I nodded. "Definitely. Stellamar feels like home now."

"I like hearing you say that." Dad shook the spices into his meatball mixture. "I wasn't so sure when we first moved."

"Me either," I admitted. "I'm not big on change." I turned to the stove and shook the linguine out of the box and into the boiling water in the big red pot. Lady Azura's pot, I realized. We shared everything now. Even though Dad and I lived upstairs on the second and third floors, we always ate together down here with Lady Azura. I stirred the pasta with a spoon we'd brought from California. Our worlds had combined. Pretty weird, since I'd only found out at Christmas time that Lady Azura is actually my great-grandmother. I never knew she existed before then.

Dad heated a pan for his meatballs, and I shifted to the side, as if we'd practiced our moves. We'd been cooking dinner together since I was old enough to tear the lettuce for a salad. Me and Dad. Sara and Mike Collins. It had always been the two of us. Now it seemed odd that Lady Azura wasn't here. Two had become three.

"Where is she?" I asked. I heard a faint creaking from across the house.

"Resting in her room. I said we'd call her when the feast was ready. Her last client left half an hour ago." He dropped the meatballs into the sizzling pan. "They're keeping her busy!"

"Too busy. She's always tired."

"Sara, she's very old. Old people get tired."

"She's not an *old* person," I protested. "At least, she never used to act like one. She stayed up all night. She never used to rest."

"She's making a lot of money," Dad pointed out.

"You always say that money isn't everything," I countered. "I liked it better when she had barely any clients. We haven't had our lessons in weeks."

"Is something wrong? Do you need to talk to her about . . . uh . . . about stuff?" Dad's forehead wrinkled with concern.

It had taken him years to grasp that I could see the dead. When he finally did, he'd moved us across the country. He knew Lady Azura could do it too. It's a family thing on my mom's side. Lady Azura had been giving me lessons, teaching me how to control the ghosts and how to develop new powers.

"If you want, I could try to help," he offered. He

worked hard to hide it, but I knew paranormal stuff made him uncomfortable. Or nervous. Or both.

"Everything's fine," I assured him. "Nothing too spooky going on." I smiled at him, and he smiled back.

Floorboards groaned overhead. Footsteps paced. I ignored them. Just the usual spirits moving about our house. Mr. Broadhurst with the thick mustache on the second floor was the pacer. Back and forth all the time. The sad woman who sat in the rocking chair in the pink bedroom was always rocking. She still cried about the loss of her son, Angus, who'd died when he was a baby. I talked to her sometimes. It had taken a while, but I think she'd learned to trust me. I liked her. There were six spirits in total who hung about the house. They had been here when I arrived, and I suspected they would be here forever.

"It's summertime. Lots of the clients are tourists. They'll be gone when the weather cools, and life will go back to normal for you and Lady Azura," Dad said. "Until then, you have me."

"We could look for shells tomorrow," I suggested. "I need more for the wind chimes I'm making."

"I'm here for other things too, Sara." He stopped

flipping the meatballs and stared meaningfully at me. "Not just the fun stuff like going to the beach. Though we can definitely do that tomorrow. . . ."

A drawer slammed somewhere. Then another. Drawers only I could hear.

He was trying. He wanted to understand, to help. I knew he probably couldn't, but the fact that he *wanted* to so badly meant the world to me.

"Thanks, but do you know how to block hostile spirits who won't stop asking for help?" I asked.

Dad's blue eyes widened. "Is that happening now?'

I smiled. "No. Just an example."

He exhaled loudly. "Point taken. I'm here if you need me, though. Okay, kiddo?"

"Got it, Daddy-o," I replied, using my childhood nickname for him. "Pasta's ready."

Dad dumped the linguine into the colander in the sink as I listened to a door slam. Another drawer closed. Then the squeaking of door hinges. All the noises came from down the hall, but no spirits that I knew of lived on the first floor.

Dad poured sauce over the steaming pasta. He didn't react to the sounds.

Bam! Crash!

My skin prickled. Something odd was going on.

"I'm going to get Lady Azura for dinner," I offered.

The narrow hallway from the kitchen at the back of the house led toward Lady Azura's rooms and the sitting room at the front. I took a few steps, then stopped.

Boom! Something heavy hit the floor.

I gulped. This was definitely not the usual activity in the house. I needed to tell Lady Azura.

My flip-flops slapped against the wooden floor as I hurried toward the thick purple velvet curtain that marked the entrance to her fortune-telling room. Through that room was her bedroom.

A crinkling, then the rapid flip of paper made me stop outside the opened French doors leading into the sitting room. Was someone in here?

I peered around the door, and my breath caught in my throat.

A man!

A man sat on the sofa, flipping through a large coffee-table book. Other books were strewn on the floor. A vase lay shattered. Drawers were open, their contents hanging out.

Who is he? Who is he? I stood frozen in the doorway. There was a stranger in our house!

I knew I should run away. Stranger danger and all that, yet all I could do was stand and stare.

"Get out," I ordered, my voice no louder than a whisper. "Get out!"

The man ignored me. Instead he leaned back on the pale teal sofa cushion and propped his scuffed brown leather shoes, one by one, on the polished wood table.

Lady Azura would go crazy if she saw his feet on her furniture. Absolutely crazy. A scream pushed up through my body, stopping at the base of my throat.

"This is not your house!" I cried in a voice much quieter than I intended. I had wanted to scream. "Get out!"

The man turned toward me. He was old, probably in his seventies. His white shirt had a yellow stain by the collar, and he was mostly bald. His eyes held a milky, faraway gaze. "I am a guest. An invited guest."

A guest? What was he talking about?

I turned and finally ran. Racing through the darkened fortune-telling room, I pushed open the second curtain leading into Lady Azura's bedroom.

All the shades were drawn. I could make out Lady Azura sleeping on her large bed. A thin blanket covered her small body, and a black silk mask shielded her eyes. The citrusy scent of her face cream filled the air. I took a deep breath, calming myself, wondering how to wake her. Old people startle easily.

Then I heard rustling against the back wall.

The clacking of hangers.

The crinkling of tissue paper.

In the dimness, I saw the faint silhouette of a stocky woman standing in front of Lady Azura's opened closet. She bent over and tried on a pair of high heels. Lady Azura's high heels!

I gaped in surprise. The woman tossed the shoes aside and pawed through the hanging dresses.

I finally found my voice. "Lady Azura, get up."

Lady Azura gave a slight groan but kept sleeping.

The woman pulled down a hatbox.

"Stay out of there," I called. I shook Lady Azura's knobby shoulder. Her body felt so frail. "There's a woman going through your closet! She's touching your clothes!"

She woke immediately. Pushing the eye mask up

onto her head, she blinked several times, bringing me into focus.

"Look!" I pointed to her wrecked closet.

Lady Azura turned and registered the woman hunched over several shoe boxes. She brought her hands up to rub her temples but didn't speak.

"Your clothes!" I tried again. Lady Azura loved her clothes. She was one of the most fashionable women I'd seen outside a magazine. "And there's a strange man in the sitting room. He's touching everything, and he has his shoes on the furniture!"

"I see," she said calmly. She didn't jump out of bed. She didn't scream. She just sat there, watching.

"*Wait.* You're *good* with this?" I sounded hysterical. I thought that was the appropriate response when you discovered strangers going through your stuff. My head started to pound.

"No, I am not good with this." She swung her legs around and stood. She stepped toward her closet. "Eleanor? Eleanor, can you hear me?"

The woman turned, caught with two leather handbags in her arms. She looked familiar.

"Eleanor," Lady Azura continued calmly in her

low, raspy voice. "We've talked about respecting possessions."

"You *know* her?"

Lady Azura nodded. "This is Eleanor. The man in the sitting room is her husband, Dwight. They will be staying with us for a while."

"Staying with us? Who *are* they?"

"Sara, I expect you to have better manners and say hello first."

My gaze flicked between Lady Azura and the old woman still holding the handbags. She had a softness about her—round cheeks, plump body, a marshmallow cloud of white hair. She grew almost fuzzy in her softness as I stared. Suddenly I remembered her. She'd been waiting out front earlier. She and her husband. The man with the limp. They had entered the house behind the long-haired woman.

They were ghosts.

As I took a closer look, I realized that I couldn't see all of Eleanor's body. Sections shimmered, then faded in and out. Her legs were almost translucent.

As long as I have been seeing ghosts, they still sometimes catch me by surprise. Like now.

I looked to Lady Azura. She nodded in Eleanor's direction.

"Hello," I managed, even though this didn't seem the time for manners. "Why are they here?" I asked Lady Azura.

"Mrs. Merberg, my last client today, was having a rough time. She has become a magnet for the spirits of her extended family. They have all descended upon her. She can't see them, but she can feel them. The poor woman hasn't slept in days."

"What does she want you to do?" I asked. Eleanor gave me a hopeful smile. I gave her a feeble smile in return, so as not to be rude, but I definitely wasn't in the mood to act like the welcome wagon.

"She wants them gone," Lady Azura explained. "The trick is to figure out what is needed to send each one on his way. Eleanor and Dwight were Mrs. Merberg's aunt and uncle. They've been the most exhausting to her, so I offered to have them stay here until I can sort through all the issues."

"But they're *touching* everything." Eleanor was now running her hands over a pile of sweaters.

"Yes, they seem to be very nosy. Mrs. Merberg had

the same problem with them poking into everything in her house. She was not able to deal with them, but I can." Lady Azura moved alongside Eleanor. "Eleanor, you must stop. Otherwise, I cannot allow you to stay. Understand?"

Eleanor began to shake. Being scolded by Lady Azura was like being sent to the principal's office. I could feel her regret flowing out of her unstable body and into mine. "I am sorry." Her voice was muffled, as if she were speaking underwater.

I gazed at shoes spilling out of shoe boxes, silk scarves piled on the white carpet, and gauzy tops slipping off the crooked hangers. "I don't get it. You won't let me even go in your closet. You won't let *anyone* touch your personal things. How can you let them?"

"Eleanor and Dwight have been on a search since their deaths last year."

Another crash echoed from the sitting room. Dwight again.

"What are they looking for?"

"I have no idea," Lady Azura admitted, "and neither do they. I suspect that once they find it, they will be able to rest in peace. It is a mystery that must be unraveled." She gazed in dismay at the mess. "The sooner the better."

"Have you ever done this?" I asked. "Invite ghosts into your home?"

"Never under circumstances like this, but Mrs. Merberg drove up from South Carolina, because she read about me and feels only I can help her. I could not say no. I am needed."

Lady Azura couldn't hide the pride in her voice.

"I think turning our house into a hotel for ghosts is a bad idea," I said. "A very bad idea."

"Sara, you worry too much," Lady Azura chided me. "They will be good guests. Won't you, Eleanor?" Eleanor shimmered in and out focus. A sweet smile was plastered on her face, but her eyes roamed about the room.

Planning where to go next.

Lady Azura has it wrong, I thought. These ghosts were going to be trouble.

Chapter 3

"Whoa, Sara! What happened?" Lily cried as she and Buddy burst through the back door the next afternoon.

I pushed my tangled hair out of my face and surveyed the kitchen. It was worse than I'd realized.

"Come on, spill it. Wait, you already did!" Lily slapped her leg and laughed. "Get it? Spill it? Oh, Sara, you just smeared chocolate in your hair!"

"Huh?" I looked down at the melted chocolate on my hand, then felt my sticky hair. "Yikes!"

"So I repeat, what *happened*?"

Good question, I thought. But I didn't have a good answer.

"I'm baking double-double-chocolate cookies." I held up the wooden spoon dripping with dark chocolate. I'd just finished melting chocolate and butter in a double boiler.

I didn't say that while I was stirring, two ghosts had pulled out every pot, pan, and utensil in the kitchen in a frantic search. I didn't say that these same ghosts opened drawers and cabinets but had never closed them. I didn't say they'd even dug their hands into the bags of flour and sugar.

"It's a mess in here." Lily frowned and tugged Buddy's leash to keep him from cleaning the floor with his tongue. "Do you know what you're doing?"

"I totally know how to bake these. I didn't . . . I mean it wasn't me who . . ." I stopped. What was I going to say? My imaginary friends made the mess? "I like to be creative when I cook. Free-form. Experiment."

Lily leaned against the counter, eyeing me uncertainly.

"These are going to be great," I insisted. I stirred the thick chocolate until it turned smooth. "What's up?"

"I'm bored. Joey, Sammy, and Jake are at baseball practice, and Mom took Cammie food shopping. I was supposed to stay home and clean my room for the company that's coming, but Buddy and I went for a walk. Whose car is out front?"

"Repeat client for Lady Azura. The same woman

who was here yesterday." When Mrs. Merberg arrived, Eleanor and Dwight had followed her into the fortune-telling room. I was glad they were gone from the kitchen. "What company?"

"That's what I came to tell you. No, Buddy, don't lick that." She pulled Buddy away from a sprinkling of cocoa powder on the floor. "The Meyer family. They're coming tomorrow to see Buddy." She squatted next to her dog. "Aren't they, Budsters?"

"Mason, too?" I asked, hoping my question sounded casual.

Lily studied me a moment, then grinned. "You like him."

"Like who?" I measured a teaspoon of baking soda, and added it to the bowl of flour. I'd lined up all the ingredients before I'd started.

"Him. Mason. You have a crush on him!"

"Maybe. I don't know. I mean, his picture is cute, right?"

Lily jumped up. "Totally cute. You two would be so good together!"

"How do you know?" I wanted it to be true. I'd been thinking about him so much. Ever since—

"You'll look good together. You both have blond hair, and you both look sporty, even though you are kind of a spaz. It's important to look good with your boyfriend."

"We don't even know each other," I protested. "He's not my boyfriend."

"Yet." Lily clapped her hands together. "Ooh, I am totally into this. This is the first boy since Jayden that you've liked!"

I'd been crushing on Jayden Mendes all last year. Just when it seemed he liked me back and I was going to have my first real boyfriend, his parents moved his family to Atlanta. What Lily said was true. Since Jayden, I hadn't been interested in any other boys. Until Mason.

"I don't even know him," I reminded Lily. Except I did. Kind of.

I'd had visions of Mason when Buddy first showed up. I'd seen him when he couldn't see me. I'd felt something.

A connection.

The same thing had happened with Jayden—I'd had visions of him, too, before I actually met him. But my visions of Mason were different. They were some-how . . . stranger.

Lily paced the kitchen. Buddy followed. "Okay, here's the plan. When Mason and his family get to my house, I'll talk you up. You know, 'My best friend Sara is so pretty, and Sara is so creative, and Sara makes the best chocolate cookies ever and—'"

"Don't go overboard," I warned. "He'll be bummed when he meets the real me."

"I'll lose the stuff about the cookies," she joked. "Anyway, I'll build you up but not too much. Then I'll text you without him knowing. When you get it, you'll casually wander down the street. Out taking a stroll. You'll stop by my yard, and I'll introduce you, and there'll be fireworks—"

"Fireworks?"

"Like in cartoons! He'll gaze into your blue eyes and fall madly in love." Lily sighed. "It's perfect. What are you going to wear?"

"I have no idea. My red skirt? Or the striped tank dress?"

"A dress says you're trying too hard. I think you should do jean shorts and a cute top."

"What cute top? Do I have a cute top?"

Lily reviewed every top I owned. That's how close we'd become this year. She knew every piece of clothing in my closet without having to open the door.

I leaned my elbows on the counter and listened to her rank my tops from cute to not so much. My gaze settled on the big five-pound bag of sugar and its blue and yellow design.

Blue looks nice with bright yellow, I thought, staring at the bag. I wished I owned a yellow top. Yellow says sunny, happy, and fun. Mason would like a sunny girl.

All of a sudden, the heavy bag of sugar flopped onto its side. Sugar crystals cascaded onto the floor.

"Whoa!" Lily cried. She grabbed for the bag at the same time as I did. We flipped it upright. "How'd that happen?"

I glanced nervously around the room. No Eleanor. No Dwight. "No idea. It's weird."

"Buddy, no!" Lily pulled the panting dog away from the mound of sugar. Quickly I knelt down to scoop up the mess. Lily helped.

"Remind me not to have you bake my birthday

cake," Lily kidded. "You're kind of a disaster in the kitchen."

"Have you finally decided what you're doing for your birthday?" I asked. For weeks, Lily had been coming up with party ideas, loving them, then rejecting them. Indoor rock climbing. A beading workshop. A spa party. A 3-D movie.

"Not yet. What do you think about the frozen yogurt place by the lighthouse?"

"I like it, but after we eat yogurt, then what? I mean, yogurt eating doesn't take all that long." I went to the sink to get a sponge. "How about the mall?"

Lily joined me and poured water into a bowl for Buddy. "I want boys at my party too. They won't shop. All they'll do is hang at the food court."

"Tick-tock, tick-tock," I sang.

"What's that mean?"

"Your birthday is next week," I reminded Lily. "You're running out of time."

"I don't want just any party." Lily twirled a strand of her hair. It fell in waves way past the middle of her back.

"Maybe I should send out an e-mail invite today."

"An invite to what?"

"To my party at a surprise location." Lily grinned. "I like it. Kind of reverse surprise party!"

"Except even you don't know what the surprise is."

"I will. Soon—" Lily gasped. "Sara, quick, the milk!"

I whirled around. The carton of milk had fallen over. Milk spilled across the counter, waterfalling onto the floor. Buddy's nails clacked against the linoleum in his dash to lap up the white pool. Lunging forward, I grabbed the carton, stopping the flow of milk.

"How'd that spill?" Lily asked. Her brows knit together in confusion. "You and I weren't anywhere near it."

My heart thumped loudly in my chest. I searched the kitchen. Where were Eleanor and Dwight? Why couldn't I see them?

"Who are you looking for?" Lily demanded. She'd brought over a dish towel.

"No one." What could I say? "A ghost?" I offered, trying to make it sound like a joke.

"You think?" Lily's voice turned hopeful. "That would be so cool if Lady Azura called in a ghost."

"Yeah, it would." *No, it wouldn't,* I thought.

"Maybe this house is haunted. Did you ever think of that?" Lily asked.

"All the time," I admitted.

Should I tell her? Was now the time to tell her? I didn't know.

I hurried to the sink to get the sponge again. Buddy slurped the milk on the floor, but the counter was a swimming pool.

Lily's eyes shone with excitement. "It could be a ghost, or it could be some sort of other paranormal phenomena. Maybe there's some weird energy in the room that made the milk carton spill over. Stuff like that definitely happens."

I knew all about weird energy—I'd had to deal with that, too—but I was sure that the chaos in my kitchen was being caused by a spirit. It just hadn't shown itself to me. Yet.

"Actually, Lily—" A stream of icy water sprayed me in the face! I shielded my eyes with my hands. Water spurted as if by magic from the faucet. I hadn't even touched the knobs. Then I saw the hand.

A thumb covered the faucet just enough so the cold

water sprayed me. In slow motion, a body materialized. A small eight-year-old boy. Short hair tucked into a wool cap. Dark eyes filled with mischievous glee. Old-fashioned clothes.

I reached around him and turned the water off.

"Gotcha!" the boy cried. He jumped in delight. Sparks of pent-up energy prickled around his body.

Henry. The boy's name was Henry. He was one of the spirits who lived in the house. Henry was kept locked in a closet way up on the third floor, because he was trouble.

Big trouble.

What was he doing down here? I wondered.

I knew the answer immediately. Eleanor and Dwight had let him out. They'd probably opened every closet in the house by now.

There are secrets behind those doors, I thought, annoyed. *Things that need to stay hidden.*

Suddenly I sensed Lily watching me. No longer laughing. Just watching from across the kitchen.

I bit my lip and tried to think. Henry caused destruction wherever he went.

He broke things. He tore things. He'd knocked

over the sugar and spilled the milk.

Henry eyed the kitchen, plotting his next trick, unable to stay still.

Lily eyed me.

I closed my eyes. Water dripped down my face. *Think, think.* I had to get Henry out of here. But how? I couldn't talk to him. Not in front of Lily.

"Sara, what just happened with the sink? We should go get Lady Azura. I'm telling you, stuff like this happens in the movies sometimes. It's almost always something paranormal that caused it. Like a ghost, or—"

No, no, I couldn't talk about this with her right now. Not with Henry running rampant. I'd learned firsthand that he could be dangerous if he wasn't dealt with.

Henry darted across the kitchen.

What's he doing? Where's he going?

Nothing stood in his way. No pans, no pots, no spilled sugar. His feet never touched the ground.

He was heading right for Lily!

Chapter 4

I had to stop Henry!

"No!" I cried. Henry was inches away from Lily.

Suddenly he dropped to his knees. His small, shimmering hands reached out. Then he turned to me. "It's a doggie," he said, his voice a breathless whisper.

"What?" Lily asked me. "Why'd you yell?"

Buddy sprawled contentedly by Lily's feet. Henry pointed to him. His mouth formed an O of surprise. His outstretched arms twitched.

"I thought I saw a bee," I told Lily, swatting at the air. "It's gone." I hated lying. My stomach was on fire.

"May I pet the doggie?" Henry asked. He leaned closer to Buddy.

Neither Lily nor Buddy seemed to sense Henry. Buddy stayed fast asleep.

Would it be okay? I wasn't sure. I nodded ever so slightly at Henry.

He scooted even closer to Buddy. His small hand, visible only to me, tentatively touched Buddy's back. He gently rubbed the dog's brown fur. Slowly at first, then faster. Long, loving strokes. Henry's body relaxed with each stroke. The electric current around him dimmed.

Eyes closed, Buddy rolled onto his back. Henry rubbed his belly. Buddy's hind legs fluttered with delight. His stubby tail wagged furiously.

"Check out Buddy." Lily tipped her chin toward her dog. "He's awfully happy."

"What do you think he's dreaming about?" I asked nervously.

Lily's eyes gleamed. "I totally know."

"What?" Could she sense Henry?

"Mason. He's excited to see Mason tomorrow, and he's excited because he knows you're going to get together with Mason!"

"Oh, please!" Relief, fear, and my guilt snowballed together in a laugh.

"The perfect couple!" Lily singsonged. "You and Mason!"

"Stop it." I gave her a playful shove, even though I liked the thought of us together. Lily's phone buzzed. She glanced at the screen. "Mom's home already and needs me." She looked at the kitchen floor smeared with milk and sugar, the bowls of chocolate now hardening, and the open cabinets. "I'd stay and help, but I have to clean my own room. That's looking a lot easier now that I've seen your mess." She toed Buddy with the tip of her sneaker. "Time to go!"

Henry gazed up in horror as Lily clipped Buddy's leash to his collar. He wrapped his arms tightly around Buddy's neck.

Lily tugged the leash. Buddy opened his eyes but didn't move. Lily tugged again. Buddy stayed rooted to the spot. How could he move? He had a determined eight-year-old ghost holding him down.

"Buddy! Come!" Lily called. "Come!"

I bent down and pried Henry off Buddy. I tried to make it look as if I was nudging the dog. "Time to go home," I said, then pushed Buddy toward Lily and out the back door.

I shut the door before Henry could follow.

"Doggie!" Henry wailed.

"The dog will be back, but you cannot be down here," I said sternly.

I spent the next two hours dragging Henry up two flights of stairs and safely into his closet and then cleaning the kitchen. Lady Azura stayed in her room with Mrs. Merberg, Eleanor, Dwight, and who knew how many other spirits. Their session was taking way longer than usual. I stood outside the purple curtain but could only hear the murmur of Lady Azura's voice.

What are you doing in there? I wondered.

I hoped she was figuring out how to send those nosy spirits on their way, now that my best friend thought our house was haunted.

"Whatcha doin'?"

I ignored the question and folded a thin strip of paper like an accordion.

"Whatcha got there? Can I see?" Dwight leaned over me. He would've cast a long shadow in the afternoon sun, except spirits don't have shadows.

Dwight and Eleanor were still here, nosy as ever. Lady Azura hadn't been able to help them yesterday.

I ignored Dwight while I sat cross-legged on our

front porch, trying to make an amazing birthday card for Lily. It was going to be a 3-D card. Once glued in place, the folded strips of paper would make the glittery cupcake that I'd drawn and painted spring out from the background.

Dwight wouldn't stop. He opened and closed the metal mailbox hanging on the side of the porch. He lifted the welcome mat. He peeked under every piece of colored paper I had by my side.

The double swing that hung at the far end of the porch swayed slightly, even though there was no breeze. I never sat on that swing, because the knitting spirit always sat there. She never talked. She never moved. She just knit. The scarf she knit never got any longer. I used to find her creepy. Today I liked her silence.

I folded another strip and stared at my cell phone. *Buzz, already!* The Meyers' car—a white SUV with tinted windows so I couldn't see inside—had driven by my house fifteen minutes ago. Now it was parked two doors down at Lily's. I'd heard the Randazzo family exclaim and greet the Meyers. Buddy barked. Lily's brothers yelled.

I'd heard it all but couldn't see anything.

Should I get off the porch and take a peek? I wondered. I was so curious about Mason. But if I stood on our walkway, anyone in the Randazzos' yard could spot me. Our plan would never work then.

I smoothed the silky orange halter top Lily and I had chosen. Orange was bright and sunny like yellow. My straight hair lay smooth and shiny, falling just past my shoulders. I wondered if I should put on more lip gloss. I'd probably bitten it all off.

Mr. Randazzo's deep laugh floated down the street.

"What's in this box? Markers?" Dwight asked.

I didn't want to stay here, waiting by myself. I bent to gather the markers Dwight sent rolling across the porch floor.

"Hi."

Markers in each fist, I looked up. Mason stood on the bottom porch step.

Mason!

His eyes were even greener than in my visions. A deep green with flecks of gold. He smiled, and the air grew warmer. The back of my neck began to sweat.

"Hi," I said.

"Lily told me to come by. You're Sara, right?"

I couldn't understand why Lily had changed the plan, but it didn't seem to matter. He was even cuter than I had ever imagined, and I had imagined major cute. He kept smiling at me. A warm smile that made my fingertips tingle.

"Yes." I couldn't stop looking at him. Into those eyes. He stared back, unblinking. Neither of us would look away.

Neither of us could look away.

"You're very pretty," he said. "Everyone must tell you that."

I did hear that sometimes, but I wasn't sure I really believed it. But the way he said it to me, I believed it. Happiness settled over me like a shawl. Mason thought I was pretty.

I raised my fists. "Do you like art?"

"Markers aren't my thing, but I love photography. I also like to paint."

"Me too!" I exclaimed, blushing a little over his joke about markers. In addition to being totally cute, he loved art and was funny!

I told him all about the photos I took. He liked

still lifes and landscapes, too.

He moved up the steps, closer to me. Our eyes stayed connected. "Did you see the movie *Seasons*? It's a nature documentary using paintings."

"It's my all-time favorite," I exclaimed. Talking to boys usually makes me nervous. With Jayden, it took a long time for me to be able to talk to him without feeling like I was sticking my foot in my mouth every two seconds.

But it was different with Mason. I felt as if we'd known each other all our lives.

"What about—?"

"Sara, what are you doing out here?" Lady Azura interrupted. I hadn't heard her come outside.

"I'm talking to . . ." I blinked, then blinked again. I stood and scanned the porch, then the walkway. *Where'd he go? Did he hide from her?*

"It's okay," I called out. Had he ducked behind a bush?

"Who are you talking to? What's okay?" Lady Azura asked. She stood by my side and gripped my arm. Her bony fingers pressed into my flesh.

I heard Mr. Randazzo laugh again. Then I heard

Sammy Randazzo yell, "Mason, let's play keep-away with Buddy!"

Buddy barked.

Not here. There.

Mason wasn't here. I swallowed hard. He hadn't ever been here, I realized. I'd been daydreaming.

"No one," I admitted. I was embarrassed to tell Lady Azura about Mason. "I was wondering something," I said to change the subject.

"Sure." She lowered herself into the wicker chair near the front door. She was always careful not to get sun on her face.

"Lily's birthday is coming up. She loves my necklace." I reached under the high-necked halter and pulled out the cord Lady Azura had given me when I first came to Stellamar. Seven different small crystals dangled on the chain. "Do you think I can give Lily a necklace like this as a present?"

"I don't see why not. What crystal shall we start her with? What power does Lily most desire?"

I fingered the crystals around my neck. A ruby crystal for love, an aquamarine for courage, a hematite for self-confidence.

"I can choose anything?" I asked.

"Different crystals and gemstones help awaken or strengthen powers buried deep within," Lady Azura reminded me. We had talked a lot about crystals over the past several months. When I first moved here, I wasn't so sure that they could really do anything, but now I really believed in them. I knew my crystals helped me, and they were really important to me.

Suddenly I knew what to give Lily. "Is there a stone to give Lily psychic powers? You know, to make her see spirits, or have visions or something like that?"

"Why do you ask that?" Lady Azura asked suspiciously. "Does she know . . . about you?"

"No, no, not at all." Lady Azura believed I shouldn't tell Lily. She liked Lily a lot. In fact, the two of them bonded over their love of fashion. But she felt that I needed more confidence in my powers before I opened myself to judgment. Even from my best friend.

"Lily's really interested in paranormal stuff. She's always asking me about your powers, and she's really obsessed with this movie about a haunting at some old inn." I told Lady Azura about *The Haunting at the Spalding Inn* and Justin Drexler.

Lady Azura let out a deep-throated chuckle. "I admire how open minded Lily is—not everyone is like that, as you and I well know. But even the most powerful crystal cannot jump-start what is not already there."

"Do you think it's impossible that Lily might have powers too?"

Lady Azura looked at me for a long moment before responding. I think she was deciding what to say. Or how to say it. "I do not think it's impossible, but I do think it is highly unlikely. However, I can see why you might want Lily to have powers too."

"No, it's not just that," I insisted, unable to hold her gaze. And it wasn't just *me* wanting it. Lily was really interested in paranormal stuff. She had told me so many times that she wished she could do what Lady Azura can do. What I can do too.

"I do understand," Lady Azura assured me. She reached over and squeezed my hand.

"But, Sara, if it were so easy to talk with the dead, cemeteries would be as crowded as amusement parks." She let go of my hand and leaned back. "It's a nice wish for Lily to have. How about a gem that encourages wishes to come true?"

"I like that. Does it really work?" *Maybe I should get one,* I thought.

"The moonstone is a wishing stone with great mystical power. It's not a genie in a bottle. It helps focus desire," Lady Azura said. "I have a man I get my crystals from. His name is Hector. I will order the moonstone from him today."

"Thank you." I knew Lily would love it. "Maybe she can—"

A *crash*. Then another!

We both swiveled in time to see a third clay flowerpot tip off the far side of the porch. It landed with another *crash*, smashing into pieces on the driveway that ran alongside the house.

Eleanor shimmered into view. She clasped her hands to her round cheeks. "Oh, dear. They were heavier than I thought. I just wanted to take a peek under them."

I waited for Lady Azura to scold her. To tell her to leave our stuff alone. She didn't say anything, though.

"Eleanor and Dwight are out of control." I told her

about Henry getting out and the embarrassing mess in the kitchen.

Lady Azura waved her hand. "No harm was done, child."

"This time," I cautioned. "What happens if they let Henry out again? Do you remember last Halloween when he got out? It'll be worse than spilled sugar next time."

"Sara, what we do comes with risks. There are elements beyond our control. Mrs. Merberg's case is tricky and will take time. Did you know that she's a published author? She may write a book about me and this experience."

"Really? That's great! But when are Dwight and Eleanor going? How does sending them on work?" A blue sports car stopped in front of our house. The car had license plates from New York.

"Who's that?"

"She should be my next client."

"Another one?" I couldn't keep the disappointment from my voice. It had been a long time since Lady Azura and I had sat on the porch and talked.

"Busy, busy." Lady Azura stood and straightened

her long gauzy white skirt. "Are you good out here until I am done?"

I watched a thin woman with short blond hair and retro sunglasses climb out of the car. My eyes widened as three black cats followed her.

Not living cats.

Ghost cats.

Seriously? I thought. *We're adding animals to all the other spirits in our house?*

"I—" My phone buzzed the special chime I had for Lily.

Dwight peered over my shoulder at the screen.

PLAN IS A GO! MASON TIME!

This was it. I was finally going to meet Mason face-to-face.

"I'm totally fine," I told Lady Azura. "In fact, I'm going to Lily's house."

Chapter 5

The Randazzos' front yard was empty when I got there.

Had I missed him? Had they gone home?

No. The white car was still parked out front. Then I heard voices from the backyard.

I exhaled and tried to calm my nerves. *He's just a boy*, I told myself. *Relax.* I strolled around the side of their white Victorian house, just like Lily and I had planned. *Casual. Look casual,* I instructed myself. I let my arms swing at my side as I forced myself to walk slowly. *La-la, just wandering along.*

I spied Lily's parents sitting on their back deck with Mr. Meyer and his wife. The adults sipped iced tea and talked. Mrs. Meyer gestured wildly with her hands. The sun shone brightly in the cloudless sky.

Lily's three younger brothers and her little sister

played kickball with a blond boy and girl, who I guessed were the Meyers' twins. The boy pitched the red rubber ball to Sammy. Cammie cheered for her brother.

"Fetch, Buddy!" Lily cried.

I swiveled toward the far end of the large yard. Lily stood next to Mason. He threw a navy Frisbee. Buddy raced after it.

I swallowed hard.

Mason was just as cute as I'd imagined. Short, spiky white-blond hair. Honey-tanned arms and legs.

Buddy scampered back with the plastic Frisbee dangling from his mouth. Mason pried it loose and flung it again. He had a strong arm, and he stood with the confidence of an athlete.

Lily looked my way. She grinned and nodded her head wildly.

Mason kept his eyes on Buddy.

Lily moved her eyebrows up and down. She nodded toward Mason. Then she wiggled her eyebrows again.

Was that some sort of code?

Buddy whizzed back to Mason, but I stayed focused on Lily's odd twitching.

Was I supposed to come over? Or stay away?

"Watch out!" Mason yelled.

The Frisbee jerked off course and rocketed straight for my head. I knew Mason was watching me now. This was it. I leaped in what I hoped was a combination of graceful ballet and athletic force. I threw my arms out and caught it. *I caught it!* I waved the Frisbee in the air. What a great first impression!

Lily cheered.

Mason just stared at me. Frowned. Clearly not impressed.

A lump lodged in my throat. He was supposed to smile at me, not frown. That was how it'd always been in my daydreams.

"Throw it to Buddy!" he called. No "Hello." No "What's your name?" No "You are so pretty."

I flung the Frisbee toward Buddy. It spiraled lamely, then dropped only a few feet in front of me. My usual bad Frisbee throw. I scooped it up and jogged over to where they stood.

"Here." I smiled brightly and thrust the Frisbee toward Mason.

He took a step back and stared at the grass.

I hesitated. Was he moving away from me?

Lily's hand pressed between my shoulder blades and gave me a push forward. A push toward Mason. My arm was still outstretched, as if I was jousting, and unless he wanted to get pummeled in the chest by the Frisbee, Mason had no choice.

He reached out his hand, and our fingers brushed. Knuckles against knuckles.

He grabbed the plastic disc, and we stepped away. Barely a second had passed, but in that instant, the sky seemed to darken.

I looked up as Lily began introductions. Clouds had suddenly rolled in. The sky shifted from blue to steel gray in an instant. A weird weather coincidence.

"And this is Sara. I was just telling you about her," Lily was saying.

"Hi! I love your dog, Buddy," I said cheerfully.

"He's not my dog anymore." Mason watched the kickball game, refusing to meet my gaze.

"Well, he still kind of is," Lily said. "You can come visit anytime. Really! Rachel and Ben, too."

He looked at her. "Thanks. That's really cool of you."

"No problem. Hey, do you like art? Sara is incredible at crafts and photography," Lily said.

"Nah, I don't like art at all," Mason said. "I can't even draw a stick figure."

"What do you like to do?" I did more than art. We had to have *something* in common.

"I skateboard. I'm working on a double kick flip. I almost have it."

I had no idea what a double kick flip was.

"That's sweet!" Lily exclaimed. "Can you do a three-sixty?"

"Totally. Hey, have you guys seen that skateboard movie, *Renegade Rider*? It's amazing."

"No," I admitted. I'd never even heard of it. We went on to compare music and books, too. Totally opposite tastes.

How could this be? I wondered. What about our connection?

I'd felt it so strongly in the visions. Now, here, in person, Mason and I were like strangers.

"You are such a cheater!" Jake's voice rang out.

"I am not!" Sammy yelled back. "You never play by the rules. Lily! Lily!"

Lily rolled her eyes. "I'm the family referee. I'll be right back. Got to set them straight before the game gets ugly."

Lily ran off, leaving me and Mason standing awkwardly together.

I inspected the orange polish on my toes. I wasn't sure where else to look. The minty aroma of his gum reminded me just how close he was. I sensed him shifting his weight from foot to foot, unsure of what to do.

"Sara! Come play!" Cammie called to me.

I raised my head and waved. It was the perfect excuse to get away. All I had to do was join the kick-ball game. Yet I stayed, glued to the spot. Darker clouds now blanketed the sky. Shadows fell around us. Neither Mason nor I spoke.

He doesn't like me. I'd been wrong about us. So why did I have a warm feeling? That same sweaty sensation I got when I had a fever?

The game started up again. Lily played umpire by home plate. Rachel, Mason's sister, readied herself to kick. Both Mason and I watched the action.

Walk away, I told myself. *If you're not going to talk to him, just leave.*

But my body wouldn't obey. Something was going to happen, I could sense it. I always stayed in the theater after a movie finished, watching the credits roll and waiting for a secret funny scene at the very end. I'd force Lily or my dad to remain in their seats too. Lots of times the screen went black without a bonus scene, and the waiting was for nothing. But not all the time. Sometimes, something happened.

Sammy pitched the red ball across the grass, which was starting to brown in the summer heat. Rachel, tall and athletic like her older brother, pulled back her leg. Her foot connected. The ball soared into the air. Thunder rumbled.

Mason and I watched the ball arc over the outfield.

Walk away, I told myself again. *He's not the boy for you.*

I kept watching the ball. A sudden gust of wind twirled it around. The ball veered left, now barreling in our direction. If I didn't move, it would hit me.

My legs wouldn't cooperate. The yard faded into a watercolor of greens. All I could see was the red dot moving faster and faster my way.

"Hey!" Mason yelled. He dropped the Frisbee just

as the ball made another odd turn, and it fell right into his outstretched hands.

Thunder crashed. Wind shook the leaves on the branches. The first drops of rain fell. I'd never seen a ball twist and turn like that. Rain splattered my skin as the freak storm opened the skies.

"Game over!" Lily's dad called. Everyone ran for the house. Inside, a mass of noisy bodies crowded the Randazzos' kitchen, clamoring for towels and exclaiming over the sudden storm.

Lily pulled me aside. "He saved you," she whispered.

"What?"

"He saved your life. The ball was heading right for you." Her eyes sparkled. "He *must* like you."

"Oh, come on, Lil. One, my life wasn't in danger from a rubber ball. Two, he definitely does not like me. Totally dislikes me is more like it."

I wanted Lily to be right, though. I wanted Mason to like me.

There was talk about what to do now that the rain was coming down. Mason told his mom they should go home, but Rachel and Ben wanted to stay and play with Lily's brothers. In minutes, all the younger kids and Buddy ran upstairs, already planning a massive game of hide-and-seek. Mr. Randazzo led the Meyers into their family room, and Mrs. Randazzo followed with more iced tea and cookies.

Lily, Mason, and I trailed after them awkwardly.

"I'm going to take off," I whispered to Lily.

"You can't. Remember the plan?"

"What plan?" Mason asked.

"To hang out and watch movies," Lily said without hesitation, "even though Sara doesn't like spooky paranormal movies like I do."

"I hate them too," he said.

Finally we had something in common.

"You two are so lame." Lily leaned in, forcing the three of us into a huddle to hear her. Mason stared at the ground. "But listen, speaking of paranormal stuff, I have some awesome news to share."

I felt my stomach clench up. What was Lily going to say? It was almost as if Mason sensed my discomfort because he looked pretty uncomfortable himself. Lily didn't seem to notice.

"So after all that weird stuff happened in your kitchen, Sar . . ." Lily paused to fill Mason in on what she was talking about, and I frantically tried to figure out how to respond to whatever news Lily was about to share about the spirits in my kitchen.

"After all that happened I did some research into energy and vibes and stuff," Lily continued. My stomach unclenched. She wasn't going to talk about spirits. She was talking about energy. Nothing to worry about there. "Well, it turns out that it totally could have been one of us making all that stuff happen . . . like, with our minds!"

Lily looked at me expectantly.

I felt so relieved I could have hugged her on the spot.

"Lily, it was most definitely *not* me, so it must have been you!" I said in a joking tone.

"I had a feeling you'd say that." Lily grinned at me. "And who knows? Maybe I can do amazing things with my mind! Justin Drexler says in his blog that people can do anything they put their minds to. So I've been practicing harnessing the unknown powers of my mind. I'm getting really good! I can almost roll a pen without touching it."

"How?" Mason asked, suddenly looking up.

"With my mind. You can't believe the concentration it takes."

Mason didn't say anything, but I could tell from his face he thought Lily was a bit odd.

"Don't you believe in the supernatural?" she asked.

"Definitely not." He jiggled his right leg and tried to give his mom a look to hurry her along. His mom kept her full attention on a story Mr. Randazzo was telling.

"Well, you have to believe Lady Azura communicated with your dead grandmother to get your family's stolen jewelry back," Lily said.

"Eh, whatever." Mason shrugged as if he knew better.

That shrug made me angry. Did he not believe what Lady Azura could do? "That's the truth," I insisted.

"Can you actually prove it?" he countered.

Of course I could prove it. I wasn't going to, though. "Not exactly. Lady Azura could."

"She's silly," he scoffed. "Supernatural stuff is silly."

"You are so wrong. Let's go to Sara's house, and you can talk to Lady Azura. They live together, you know," Lily said.

"Really?"

"She's my great-grandmother," I said proudly. "We can go now. Do you want to meet her? She's pretty awesome, and—"

"No, thanks." He scowled at me.

Lily sensed the tension. "Guess what? Midnight Manor is reopening in a couple of days. My cousin David, who works there, says it's going to be twelve times spookier!"

"Is it still in the same spot on the boardwalk?" Mason asked. Even though he didn't live in Stellamar, everyone in the surrounding towns visited our boardwalk. We were the only one for miles with rides, arcades, and a haunted house.

"Exact same spot. They totally updated the haunted house. I'm going on opening day. Do you want to come with me and Sara?"

"Sure," Mason said.

Did he really mean that? I wondered. He definitely didn't like me. Maybe he liked Lily?

"It's a plan." Lily handed him her cell phone. "Type in your number." She nudged me. "We'll give you our numbers too."

Mason pulled his phone from the pocket of his baggy shorts and started to hand it to Lily. She crouched down to tie her shoelace, and Mason had no choice but to offer it to me.

Our pinkies brushed each other.

At that exact moment, the lights flickered throughout the house.

"Dave? Dave, where are the flashlights?" Lily's mom cried. "We're about to lose power."

The lights stayed on. The rain drummed against the gutters.

I inspected my hand. Had I done something to cause that? The familiar feverish feeling heated up my body.

We passed around phones and then stood uncomfortably. Mason looked as pained as I felt.

"Kids, come over and have some cookies and talk to us," Mrs. Randazzo called.

I tried to think of an excuse to leave, as we all moved toward the coffee table.

Then it happened.

Mrs. Meyer's tall glass, recently refilled to the brim with the sun-darkened iced tea, tipped over. The dark liquid soaked her white pants and dripped onto her gold sandals.

Everyone jumped up. Mrs. Randazzo raced to grab a dish towel. Mrs. Meyer acted like the embarrassing splotches staining the thighs of her pants weren't a big deal. It didn't take long for the Meyers to make excuses, gather their kids, and say their friendly good-byes.

The rain stopped as the Randazzo family stood in the front yard with Buddy and waved at the Meyers' retreating car. I stayed inside and gazed around the family room. The sun peeked through the large window.

Something wasn't right.

That glass hadn't spilled on its own. And that ball hadn't changed direction by itself.

There was a spirit here, somewhere. I was sure of it.

But why couldn't I see who it was?

Chapter 6

"Wow, Sara, I never realized you were such a slob! You find out new things about your best friend every day, I guess!" Lily exclaimed on Thursday afternoon.

"I'm not a slob," I said lamely. That was hard to believe. First the kitchen and now my crafts room. "Things got . . . out of control."

Actually, Eleanor and Dwight were the ones out of control.

The extra room on the third floor that Dad had painted yellow and made into my special place to create was usually so neat and organized. But not with our new house guests poking around all afternoon. Now pom-poms, sequins, foam pieces, and beads spilled from labeled containers. The floor sparkled with glitter.

Dwight and Eleanor stood arm in arm, inspecting

all the framed photographs hanging on the far wall. I hoped they wouldn't touch them. How would I ever explain moving frames?

"Is it okay if Buddy's up here?" Lily held his new blue leash.

"Yeah, it's not like he's going to make it any messier," I said.

"Are you ready?" Lily checked out my frayed jean shorts and purple tank. "You don't look ready."

"I'm good. We're just going to the boardwalk."

"But Mason's coming. He texted me. Well, I texted him and then he texted back, but same thing."

"So what? He doesn't like me."

"Don't be so negative. He's just warming up to you."

"Warm? It felt pretty cold the other day between us."

"Things will get hot, hot, hot in the haunted house!" Lily sang, rubbing her hands together and waggling her eyebrows at me.

I laughed at Lily's ridiculous gestures. "Oh, please." Could I get out of it? I didn't like haunted houses. I had enough spooky stuff here.

"Let's go," Lily said, clapping her hands, unable

to hold back her excitement. "Lucky for you, you're naturally gorgeous, so you can get away with that . . . less-than-spectacular outfit. We have to get a move on! I want to see how they spookified the place. That's what David said it was—*spookified*!"

The boardwalk was Lily's favorite place. She'd grown up alongside it, and her large family owned half the businesses there, but she never tired of the rides, the Skee-Ball, or the pizza and ice cream. Every trip to the boardwalk was an adventure. I couldn't back out.

"Almost ready," I promised. I tied one last shell onto the wind chimes. Eleanor hovered nearby, ready to dig her hands into my plastic bag of shells. I knotted it closed.

Then I made a double knot.

"Buddy, stop pulling." Lily tugged the leash. Buddy strained against her grip. "What's with you, boy?"

Buddy inched forward. His collar pushed into the fur around his neck. His tongue panted wildly. Lily loosened her hold, and Buddy scampered to the closet door. He gave a high-pitched whine, then scratched at it with his paw.

"Don't do that, Buddy." Lily yanked him back.

Buddy wouldn't leave the door. His rapid panting grew more urgent.

Lily turned to me. "What's in there?"

Panic bloomed in my lungs. "Just supplies," I said.

And the ghost of a young boy.

Buddy's whining grew louder. Lily couldn't pull him away.

"This is ridiculous." Before I could react, Lily flung open the closet door.

There stood the shimmering ghost of Henry.

I cringed, preparing for disaster.

Even Eleanor and Henry stopped peeking under the table to watch.

Henry dropped to his knees and hugged Buddy. The dog's tail swished happily. His whining and panting stopped. Henry rubbed behind his ears as Buddy curled up at his feet.

Lily yanked the cord that dangled from the ceiling. A single bare bulb lit the shelves of crafting supplies my dad had just installed in the small walk-in closet. "Buddy, what's wrong with you? There's nothing here."

"Maybe he likes the smell of glue," I offered.

"I thought maybe he sensed something in your

house." Lily sounded disappointed.

"Sensed what?"

Otherwordly things. I've read that dogs are some-times really in tune with paranormal stuff. I thought maybe Buddy was, and he was sensing something. But I think you're right . . . it's probably just the glue."

I was trying to figure out how to respond to that when my dad poked his head in the room, providing the perfect distraction.

"Hey, Mr. C.! I like your new haircut!" Lily grinned at my dad.

"My summer look." My dad patted his closely cropped sandy curls. "I get sheared in the summer. Just like you, Buddy boy." He bent down to pat Buddy's furry head.

For a moment, my dad's and Henry's hands rested side by side.

"Lily and I were going to the boardwalk. Midnight Manor just reopened," I said. "Is that okay?"

"What about this mess?" His brows knit together, deepening the crease between his eyes.

"I promise I'll clean it when I get home. Really and truly." I crossed my heart with my finger.

"Okay, kiddo. Deal. What about Buddy boy here?"

"I have to watch him today," Lily said.

"A haunted house is no place for a dog. I'm doing some repairs around here before dinner. How about you leave Buddy with me? I could use a canine assistant."

"Wow! That would be great." Lily offered my dad the leash.

"No!" Henry wailed. A voice only I could hear.

"One sec," Dad said to Lily. "Let me change out of my office clothes. I'll be back for Buddy boy." He hurried down to his bedroom on the second floor.

Lily turned to me. "I'm going to use your bathroom. Watch Buddy, okay?"

"Sure." I grabbed Buddy's leash as Lily headed downstairs.

"Doggie!" Henry cried again. He wrapped his arms protectively around Buddy. Buddy's tail wagged.

I had no idea whether Buddy could see Henry, but the dog definitely knew Henry was there. And Henry was so calm with Buddy.

Could I let Henry hang out with Buddy and my dad? I wouldn't be gone too long, and Henry would be so happy.

No way. It would be crazy to leave mischievous Henry out with no one to watch him.

But he'd have a meltdown if I tried to get him back inside the closet.

What to do? Lily and Dad would be back soon.

That was when I spied Eleanor running her hands over my computer keyboard. That was when I had my great idea.

The line to get into Midnight Manor snaked all the way to the arcade.

"We've been here twenty minutes and barely moved," Miranda Rich complained to us as we arrived and took our place in line behind her. Avery Apolito, Luke Goldberg, Garrett Moscato, and Nate Liu stood together toward the middle of the line.

"I'm talking to David." Lily hurried to find her cousin, who was working at the haunted house this summer.

The rest of us watched the tourists line up to play games of chance.

"That one's new," I said, pointing to the nearest booth. A teenage boy with shaggy hair and a peeling sunburn monitored a softball toss. Three milk bottles were stacked in a pyramid atop a platform. The object was to knock all three bottles down with one throw of the ball.

"I've been watching it," Luke reported. "It doesn't seem like a trick. You just have to whack the bottles at the right spot to make them all fall."

We discussed strategies. Many games on the boardwalk were designed to be nearly impossible to win. We all knew the darts had blunt tips and the balloons were underfilled, making the chance of popping them almost zero. And we stayed away from the basketball throw, because the hoops were slightly oval instead of round. No way a ball was going in.

"Look at that big green bear!" Avery squealed, waving at the grand prize hanging from the ceiling of the softball-toss booth. "That's probably the best prize on the boardwalk."

"That's not one of the cheapo ones," Luke agreed.

"Look how cute its face is!" Avery exclaimed. "And it's even bigger than I am."

"Maybe we should hang you up as a prize," Garrett teased.

"I'd be an excellent prize." Avery was at least six inches shorter than all of us, but she didn't care. She was a gymnast, and gymnasts needed to be tiny to do all those flips.

"Hey, there." Mason had appeared along with Lily.

"Hi," I said. Was he in a better mood today?

"David said we need to wait a while, but then he can get us in. Everyone, this is Mason." Lily introduced the group.

"Aves, I can win you that bear," Miranda boasted.

"No, you can't," Luke said.

"Have you ever seen her pitch a softball?" I asked. "Miranda has a killer arm."

"The game is about aim, not about force," Luke retorted.

"Let's do it!" Miranda said. She loved a challenge.

"You're on," Luke agreed.

We all followed them to the booth. Nate stayed behind to hold our place in line.

Luke went first. The big green bear could only be won by knocking down all three bottles three times in a row. Lily darted away from my side, leaving Mason next to me. She grinned meaningfully.

Mason stood stiffly with both hands shoved deep in the pockets of his cargo shorts. A black canvas backpack hung over his left shoulder. He smelled like tropical sunblock. He and Lily had been talking about the beach before. Now he was silent. He seemed as uncomfortable as I felt. I wanted to say something but couldn't figure out what.

Luke didn't hit any bottles. Garrett and Miranda teased him.

"Game's harder than he thought," I said to Mason.

"Yeah."

I couldn't stop stealing secret glances at him. He was so cute! But how could he be so different than I'd imagined? So cold?

"That green teddy bear is awesome. My dad once won me a big animal on the boardwalk, but this one's much nicer." I was babbling, but at least I was trying. "They'd look cute side by side in my room."

"I guess." Mason checked out the bear, then turned his attention back to the milk bottles.

Why did being near him make my skin heat up so much? As much as I had liked Jayden, even he never made me feel this way.

And I wasn't entirely sure I even liked Mason.

Garrett managed to knock down the bottles once. Everyone joked about the tiny stuffed seahorse that he won. Miranda whipped the softball and flattened the bottles twice. She was better than Lily, Avery, Garrett, and Luke.

"No big bear yet. So, so close. You guys got another thrower?" The teen boy, with SHERM printed on his name tag, nodded his chin toward Mason. "You look like you have a strong arm, dude. Care to prove it?"

"Come on, Mason. You try." Lily placed a dollar on the counter for him.

"Lily, it's fixed. He can't do it," Luke said.

"He totally can. Mason is awesome!" Lily exclaimed.

I could feel Mason's hesitation.

Garrett handed him a softball. "Let's see what you got."

Mason slipped off his backpack and shifted the ball between his hands, weighing his decision. Then he turned and looked at me. His piercing green eyes searched for something.

My skin flamed. Our eyes met. I nodded my encouragement.

Mason twisted back, eyed the target, and let the ball rip. The milk bottles all clattered to the ground. Direct hit!

Lily, Avery, and I cheered.

"Beginner's luck," Luke muttered. He always thought he was the best athlete around.

Sherm tossed a mini prize on the counter and handed Mason a second ball. Once again, Mason nailed the bottles. Two in a row!

He reached for the third ball.

Miranda and Luke watched cautiously. They were both extremely competitive.

"You can do it! You can do it!" Lily chanted. Avery and Garrett joined in.

I locked eyes with the big green bear dangling above the bottles. Could Mason really do it? Suddenly I wanted him to win more than anything.

He wound up, then let the ball fly. It knocked the bottom left bottle. That bottle and the top bottle toppled over, but the right bottle remained upright.

"We tied," Miranda said.

My heart sank. I stared at the lone bottle. Why couldn't it have fallen over?

My back prickled as if a heat rash was spreading under my shirt. Hot. Itchy. I looked at the green bear's embroidered smile. I wished I could've taken it home.

And then . . . and then . . .

The bottle began to sway.

Slightly at first. Then faster. Back and forth. An invisible earthquake shaking its foundation.

The bottle tipped, then fell. The clank echoed far out into the Atlantic Ocean. Everyone cheered. Garrett clapped Mason on the back.

Lily looked a bit shaken. "Wow!" she breathed.

Sherm shook his head in disbelief. "Wicked, man. I've never seen that happen before."

Mason smiled, accepting all his congratulations.

I stood apart. Was it a freak of nature that caused the bottle to fall? A slight breeze? A tremor below the ground?

"Hey." Mason appeared in front of me. The huge green bear grinned blankly from his arms. He suddenly looked really shy. "Here," he said, extending the big bear to me.

"Wait. For me? Why?" I asked.

"You wanted it. You *really* wanted it, didn't you?"

Did I?

Had I done something? I wondered. Something supernatural?

Chapter 7

"Hurry up!" Nate waved his arms over his head to get our attention. "David's letting us in."

Quickly we squeezed into the front of the line. Lily couldn't stop talking about how the bottle fell. I couldn't listen. A whirlwind of supernatural possibilities tore through my brain.

The bear rested heavily in my arms.

Had I somehow called up a spirit to knock down the last bottle? Bits and pieces of conversation swirled around me. Mason and Luke compared major-league pitching stats behind us.

A haunting melody floated out from Midnight Manor. The tune was different from the eerie one playing last summer. From the outside, the house looked different too. It had been painted black with bloodred trim. The rickety wooden sign had been replaced with neon, flashing MIDNIGHT MANOR—YOUR SCREAM AT THE BEACH.

I shifted the huge bear from arm to arm and glanced back at Mason. He ignored me, busy talking with Luke.

He just won me this prize, but now he won't look at me. I don't get it, I thought.

"I need to tell you something," Lily whispered in my ear.

What? I mouthed.

"A secret." She glanced about nervously. Avery and Miranda discussed mix-and-match bikinis in front of us. Luke and Mason added Nate and Garrett to their baseball debate.

"Spill," I whispered. I held up the green bear to block us from the others.

"It's kind of a big deal. I don't know what you're going to think." Lily seemed unsure of herself. That never happened.

"No judgment," I promised.

"Hey, Lil, pay attention. Line's moving!" David called from the door of Midnight Manor. "Everyone pair up. You need to go through two by two." He pointed to a small red light above the door. It flashed when it was time for the next couple to enter.

"Later," Lily whispered to me. "In private."

"Sure."

"Collins, what is that curious circus creature you're carrying?" David asked. His brown curls poked out the sides of his black Midnight Manor baseball cap. He gave me a crooked, teasing grin. I'd met Lily's cousin David last summer. He was supercute, but we were just friends. Plus, he was two years older.

"This is not a circus bear," I announced. "He is a fierce predator of the forest."

"Ooh, scary! Is your Emerald Forest friend going to be your partner inside?" David laughed. "If I recall correctly, you are a huge chicken when it comes to this haunted house!" I pretended to be mad at his comment and stuck my tongue out at him.

"No way. Sara and Mason are going through together. You, dear cousin, will need to provide bear-sitting services." Lily moved the bear from my arms to David's and then, as if performing a choreographed dance, pushed Mason next to me and slid into place beside Luke.

"Wait—" I began.

"No time, Sara. Line's moving." Lily grinned and nudged me from behind. Avery and Miranda had already entered together.

"I don't bear-sit," David protested. "I have a job here."

"You can use an assistant," Lily teased.

"Very funny." David turned to give me back the bear.

"Light's blinking. Your turn, Sara and Mason," Lily announced, then twisted to David. "She'll retrieve Junior when she gets out."

Mason and I stepped through the huge door and into the haunted house. The summer sun gave way to a chilling, blinding darkness. I stopped, unable to see. Cold air blew down on me. I shivered.

"What now?" Mason asked. He stood to my right.

"I— I— I don't know," I stuttered. Haunted houses made me nervous. Standing in a haunted house with a boy made me extra nervous.

"There's a lit-up arrow over there. It's pointing around a bend," Mason said. His voice sounded strained. Was he nervous too?

"Let's go." I had a plan. We'd go through the haunted house superfast. No stopping to get scared. No stopping for ghosts—real or fake. In and out, like ripping off a Band-Aid.

The narrow passageway forced us to move with our shoulders nearly touching.

"Do you want to go first?" I offered.

"Nah. You can."

Neither of us ventured forward. We stayed squished side by side. Everything was quiet. Eerily quiet. I could hear Mason breathing. Again I was close enough to smell his minty gum. Electric candles were scattered about, casting small pools of dim light.

We turned the corner and entered what looked to be an old living room. Cobwebs covered antique lamps and a swaying chandelier. The chipped keys of a grand piano moved up and down, played by unseen hands.

Mason grabbed my wrist and pointed to the framed oil portrait of a bearded sea captain above the fireplace. The eyes blinked. I sucked in my breath. The painting was alive.

Chills tingled my neck.

Just a trick, just a trick, I repeated to myself.

I hated being this scared.

Suddenly the top of the grand piano flew open. A mummy popped out. Dirty bandages crusted with gore hung from his outstretched arm. One eyeball dangled from its socket. He groaned and reached for us.

Mason tightened his grip on my wrist and pulled me out of the room.

"It's just a trick," I said. "Just a trick." I wondered if he could hear my heart boom in my chest.

"Totally. I know." He let go of my wrist. "That kid said you were chicken, though, so I was just trying to help."

We were in another dark hallway. A thin stream of cold air tickled my shoulders, as if someone stood behind me blowing. I glanced back. I couldn't see anyone.

"This way." Mason quickly followed the hallway into a large formal dining room. A half-eaten meal lay abandoned on an enormous table. Skeletons sat in all the chairs but two.

"Come eat with us," a deep voice cried.

I hesitated. "I don't think we have to stop," I said quickly. "Unless you want to?"

"Sit!" the voice commanded.

"Hey, the food looks fresher than my school cafeteria's food," Mason said.

"Totally," I agreed, not wanting to act like a big scaredy-cat.

We sat next to each other in oversize wooden chairs. Body parts floated in the platters of food. A stray tooth. A severed finger. Was that an ear? I started to gag.

Then I couldn't breathe. A tightness around my chest squeezed my lungs. What was happening?

"Get off! Get off!" Mason cried.

I tried to look at him, but I couldn't turn. I couldn't move. Something was holding me down.

A snake! A ten-foot-long snake was wrapped around my chest, binding me to my chair! Its scales were a mixture of yellow and gray. This was no trick. This snake was real.

Way real.

Tighter and tighter, it squeezed around me like a rubber band.

Mason thrashed alongside me, fighting off a snake of his own. My snake focused its menacing yellow eyes, and I began to scream. Mason screamed too.

And then I could breathe again.

The snake loosened its hold. In seconds it magically disappeared back into the arms of the chair.

Gone. A trick after all. Our screams must've made it retract, I realized.

I stood, feeling foolish. My legs shook.

Mason breathed rapidly. "Cool, huh?"

"Not really." I no longer cared if I seemed like a big chicken. I just wanted to finish and get out. Another flashing arrow appeared, sending us down a different hallway. Hands reached from the darkness. Cackling laughter echoed in the small space. Fog descended. A curtain of sticky cobwebs blocked our path. I moved as fast as I could, dodging the avalanche of scares.

Mason kept pace. Room after room. Coffins with bodies. Zombies. Then a hallway that never seemed to end. The ceiling dropped lower, until our hair nearly skimmed it. The space grew narrower. We pushed up against each other.

Thunder rumbled somewhere in the distance. A sound effect or a real storm? I couldn't tell. The electric candles flickered.

Cool air tingled along my shoulders. I whirled around. Darkness.

"Did you feel that?" I whispered.

"What?" Mason rasped. His arms were crossed over his chest. He rocked slightly from front to back.

"Like someone blowing."

"Here? There's no room in here for anyone else. There's no room in here for us."

"Let's go," I said. I was scared, but Mason sounded more than scared. Weird. Panicked. We inched our way forward in the darkness.

Mason took short, rapid breaths. He sounded as if he were fighting for air.

"Are you okay?" I stopped.

Something was wrong.

"Fine," he rasped. "Come on."

Goose bumps covered my body as cool air once again danced down my neck. I whirled around.

And saw her.

Just slightly. The shimmering outline of a girl a few years older than me. She was wearing an old-fashioned-looking dress. Something about her face wasn't right, but I couldn't see her clearly.

She wasn't a trick. She was a ghost. A real ghost who was following me.

She smiled as we locked eyes. Not a happy smile. The grin a cat gets when she spies a mouse. And then I heard her speak.

"You can see me? Well, come here, pretty girl," she called, beckoning me with her shimmering hand.

Something about her terrified me. The snakes coming out of the chair to suffocate me seemed tame compared to her.

"Hurry!" I grabbed Mason's arm to pull him forward. We stumbled in the darkness. Through a narrow hallway, away from her. Into a room that was a little less dark.

I realized the ghost wasn't following us. We were safe. I turned to say something to Mason to try and downplay my minor freak-out and saw that he seemed to be having a really hard time breathing. "What's wrong?" I asked.

"Nothing," he wheezed.

There was no way our little run through the hallway had winded Mason this much. Something was really wrong.

We had to get out of here now. Mason needed a doctor.

"A door!" I cried, spotting a door backlit in the distance. We ran for it. EXIT blinked above it.

Almost there. We were almost there.

Suddenly skeletons dropped from the ceiling. A mass of limbs blocked our path. I tried to push them aside but couldn't. They were heavier than they looked.

Mason hunched forward, hands on his thighs. He didn't move to help. Through the web of bones, I saw the sign over the door. It now flashed NO EXIT.

Mason's breathing grew even more labored.

He has to get out. He has to get out.

I didn't know which way to turn or what to do. I let out the loudest scream I could.

Other screams echoed simultaneously around me, pulling my voice into a high-pitched chorus of fear. At that very moment, screams played over and over on the sound system. My voice was drowned out completely.

Mason has to get out.

I stared at the skeletons, unable to wait until they would be lifted on pulleys back to the ceiling. I wanted them gone now. *Now!*

With a crash, the skeletons tumbled to the ground as if pulled by an invisible hand. Bones clattered and cracked in an avalanche.

I stared openmouthed. The bone blockade was now gone. The recorded screams cut off. A bell rang. Not a scary sound. A warning bell. Then the overhead lights turned on. I blinked rapidly, adjusting my eyes.

Mason's raspy gasps made me focus on the door. NO EXIT.

Was that true?

"Follow me," I ordered, stepping over the skeletal fallout.

Was this even a real door? Would it open?

I grasped the doorknob and twisted.

Chapter 8

The door opened.

I fell into in a small room designed to look like an old screened-in back porch. Mason stumbled out at my heels. A girl with red hair sat in front of an antique table selling Midnight Manor T-shirts and baseball caps. She grinned at me with plastic vampire fangs. "Vould you vant a Scream-at-the-Beach souvenir?"

"What did you do?" David banged through another door. The familiar noises of the boardwalk came from beyond it. His cheeks flushed red, as if he'd sprinted around from the ticket stand. "What did you do?"

"Nothing," I said.

"Nothing," Mason wheezed. He unzipped his backpack and rummaged about. He pulled out a small inhaler, placed it in his mouth, and took a deep breath. "Asthma," he managed when he saw our curious stares.

That explained why he couldn't breathe, I realized. He'd been having an asthma attack.

"One of you must have pulled down those skeletons in there!" David balled his hands into fists. "There is no way they just fell down! How did you do that? *Why* did you do that?"

"Not me," I said.

"I didn't touch it." Mason's breathing sounded better.

"They just dropped," I said. "That's the truth."

"Weird," David muttered. He opened the door leading back to the narrow hallway. "Pete? You fixing that?"

Mason took another breath with his inhaler, then tucked it away in his backpack.

"That was superscary," I said as we stepped outside. The humid sea air felt great against my face. I inhaled the sugary sweetness from the fudge shop across the way. "I'm never going in there again."

Mason shrugged. "It wasn't so bad."

"Seriously? I heard you scream."

"Just getting into it. I didn't want you to be the only one screaming."

"What about your asthma? My aunt Charlotte has asthma attacks when she's panicked."

Mason's eyes flashed. "I'm not your aunt Charlotte. It was that fog machine. I couldn't breathe with that. And I don't like small spaces. I was so *not* scared."

I didn't believe him, but I didn't want to argue. So far, Mason and I had never agreed on anything.

Avery and Miranda were waiting for us. Lily, Luke, Garrett, and Nate hurried out a minute later. "They cut it short," Luke grumbled. "Something broke down."

"It was so good, right? Epic scary," Lily gushed. "I am definitely coming back. I need to finish it."

We dissected the different scares as we made our way through the crowds toward the pink-and-white awning of Scoops. Lily's uncle Paul owned the popular ice-cream shop. He wasn't technically her uncle, just a close family friend, but the Randazzos all called him "uncle." Lily had so many uncles and cousins that I guessed they figured why not add one or two more.

The eight of us squeezed into a booth made for six. I was wedged between Lily and the tiled wall. Mason ended up across from me.

"It's a good thing Sara gave Junior to David," Lily

said. "Otherwise, it would be un-bear-ably tight." We all groaned at her joke.

"Why'd you do that?" Mason asked me. I couldn't read his expression. Was he upset that I didn't have the bear? Had giving it to me really meant something?

"I'm going back for my bear, whose name is not Junior, later," I assured him.

Lily shifted to talk with the others about Midnight Manor, leaving me and Mason facing each other. I pointed to the flavors printed on the blackboard. "Look," I said, "they have one called Bear Paws. Lots of brownie pieces, caramel, and nuts in it."

"Too much stuff," he replied. "That's not an ice-cream lover's flavor."

"I love ice cream, and I like Bear Paws," I replied.

"You might think you're an ice-cream lover, but you're not really. Ice-cream lovers are purists. Vanilla. Chocolate. Strawberry. No stuff in it."

"There's stuff in strawberry ice cream," I said.

"What?"

"Strawberries." I grinned.

Mason didn't grin back. "One fruit doesn't count. The rule is you can't clog up a good vanilla or a good chocolate with tons of random stuff."

"What rule?" I asked. "Who makes the rules? You?"

"No, not me. Everyone knows the rules."

"Not in Stellamar. I bet Bear Paws is one of the most popular flavors here," I countered.

"Your town's ice-cream taste is corrupt then. You need to get back to basics." He gave me a smug smirk.

"You've got to be kidding!" My voice came out much louder than I'd planned. Everyone stopped talking and stared.

Avery reached around Lily and tapped my shoulder. "I'm going to the bathroom. Want to come?"

I knew she was trying to save me. Mason was being a pain. He still flashed that smug grin, like he was smarter than us. But for some reason, I wanted to keep talking to him. I wanted to be near him. I had that same warm feeling under my skin that I'd felt when I first saw him. I didn't know what it meant, but I wanted to find out. "I'm good, Aves, thanks," I said.

The waitress came by and took our orders. I ordered Bear Paws. I had to.

"I just had the best idea!" Lily squealed. "I'm going to have my birthday party at Midnight Manor. How awesome will that be? Maybe David can get his boss to close it down just for my party. And you're all invited!"

Everyone agreed it was a great idea. We'd go to Scoops afterward, and then the girls would sleep over at Lily's. Miranda and Avery threw out suggestions as the waitress placed big glass bowls with our ice cream in front of us.

Immediately, hands shot in all directions. Scoops kept all the toppings on the tables. You could take as much as you wanted. I reached for the chocolate sauce.

"Pass the caramel," Mason said.

"Toss me the crushed cookies," Luke called.

"Sprinkles, please," Avery said. "The colored ones, not the chocolate ones."

"I call them jimmies," Nate replied.

"What's that mean? They're sprinkles, 'cause you sprinkle them." Avery laughed loudly.

"Pass the caramel," Mason said again. His request was drowned out by our loud voices as we reached for topping after topping. His hand stretched toward the bottle, but it remained barely out of range.

I wanted to help, but the caramel was too far away from me, too.

"Hey—" I started to call to Luke, who sat on the other side of Mason and was closest to the bottle. I stopped when the bottle moved.

All by itself.

Centimeters only.

Barely anything.

But it moved right into Mason's hand.

By itself.

I glanced around the table. Had anyone else seen? Everyone was digging into their ice cream. No one cared about a bottle of caramel sauce.

Mason poured the caramel onto his vanilla ice cream. He didn't seem aware of what had just happened.

I had seen it move. I knew I had. But I couldn't explain how.

The room began to sway, and a wave of dizziness rolled over me. I stared at my melting ice cream, trying to push back the sudden nausea. My arms prickled with unseen heat rash. Was I sick? Was that why I was seeing things?

"You okay?" Mason asked, leaning toward me. Was he actually concerned? He sounded concerned.

I raised my eyes. At the end of the table, the shimmery figure of a boy in short pants and a cap came into view. He raised up on his toes and waved at me.

"Henry!" I cried, attempting to stand to see him better. The tabletop of the booth stopped me.

I couldn't believe it. Henry was here. Out of my crafts room. Out of the house. On the boardwalk.

In Scoops.

"Who's Henry?" Mason asked.

My brain did backflips. Had Henry moved the bottle? How long had he been here?

"The doggie!" Henry cried. His voice was thin, barely audible above the clatter of spoons and laughter.

Dog? Oh no! Where was Buddy?

"The doggie . . . he went bye-bye," Henry said. He waved his sticklike arms. He was clearly upset.

"Henry!" I didn't know what else to say. Had he let Buddy out onto the crowded boardwalk too?

"Who is Henry?" Mason asked again.

"Yeah, Sara, who are you talking to?" Miranda added.

"I need to go. Now." I gave Lily a nudge to move her and Miranda and Nate out of our side of the booth.

"Henry is, uh—" I stood in the aisle now, inches away from the ghost boy. "He's a family friend."

"Really? Here in Stellamar?" Lily asked. She prided herself on knowing almost everyone in our town. "I never heard you mention him before."

"He's Lady Azura's friend." That was true. Sort of. Henry certainly wasn't my friend. Not now, at least. "I just saw him outside. I need to say hi, help him find his way back to our house. He gets lost easily." I was rambling and I knew it, but I had to get out of there. And bring Henry with me.

Henry tried to scoot around me, but I blocked his path.

"What about your ice cream?" Avery asked.

The last thing I wanted was the thick scoop of Bear Paws. I pulled a five-dollar bill from my pocket and pushed it onto the table. "I'm full. I need to go home. See everyone later. Got to catch up with Henry!" I waved, then tried to discreetly push Henry out onto the boardwalk with me.

Henry flailed his arms. He didn't want to be pushed. And there was nothing solid for me to hold on to. He flung over a bowl of gummy worms on one table, then knocked a container of chocolate crunchies on another. Candy scattered to the floor. Even though my back was turned, I felt Lily giving me a weird look. There was nothing to do but keep walking. I certainly wasn't going to confess that I was trying to corral a runaway ghost.

Out on the boardwalk, I cornered Henry near the funnel-cake stand. Bubbly grease mixed with the sweet smell of powdered sugar. Only three people stood on line. I tried not to move my lips as I spoke to Henry.

"Where's Buddy? Is he lost?" I couldn't imagine how I would explain losing Buddy to Lily. Or her family. Or Mason.

Henry took a step forward, his eyes finding the swirling lights of the rotating Ferris wheel down the pier. I blocked his path. "Where is Buddy?" I repeated.

"Doggie went with your daddy . . . out . . . they went out." Henry reached sideways and swiped a hunk of powdered sugar off a small girl's funnel cake, causing a mini white blizzard to explode at her feet. Tears rolled down the girl's cheeks. Her mother hurried to her rescue, bringing the pastry back for a second coating and warning her daughter to be more careful.

"So Buddy's with my dad?" I asked. I needed to be sure.

"Yes . . . I came to find my doggie."

I exhaled. Buddy wasn't lost. That was huge. I narrowed my eyes at the ghost boy. "How'd you get out?"

"The door was open." He darted around me and across the boardwalk. I hurried after, weaving my way through a family on vacation, keeping my eyes all the time on his translucent body.

"Henry! Stop!" I yelled.

He halted in front of Midnight Manor. He stared in wonder at the neon sign.

"Eleanor left the crafts room closet door open?" I asked. It didn't really matter. He was here. He was out, but I still wanted to know.

"And the front door!" His squeaky voice was filled with glee.

I groaned. My great idea had been to make Eleanor Henry's babysitter. I'd figured if she was staying with us anyway, she might as well be useful.

Bad idea. I could see that now.

"We're going back," I announced. I tried to sound forceful.

"Hey, Sara!" I spun around. David waved to me from the ticket stand. "Your bear's cramping my style."

I made my way over. Henry stayed put, transfixed by the outside of the haunted house.

"Thanks," I mumbled, reaching for the stuffed animal.

"Hey, you're not mad, are you?" asked David.

"Mad?" I watched Henry take a step backward.

"About in there. Me yelling. I didn't want to lose my job," David explained.

"No worries," I said, distracted. A man with the most enormous belly walked in front of Henry, completely blocking my view. That was dangerous. "Thanks for watching Bear. I need to go, okay?"

I hurried away. I felt as if I were always running away from people. But what choice did I have?

I managed to grab on to Henry's shimmery hand. I held tight, not sure how we were attached and afraid to let go. Marching down the boardwalk and heading back home on Beach Drive, I dragged a gigantic stuffed animal in one hand and the ghost of a boy in the other.

Chapter 9

I was angry when I finally found Lady Azura, and I don't really get angry very often. Lily always says it's weird that I never yell and scream. I always tell her that's just not me. But today I thought I might scream. Just a little.

"Eleanor and Dwight are a menace!" I exclaimed, pushing back the curtain to Lady Azura's fortune-telling room.

She sat in her large armchair, shuffling through a deck of tarot cards. "Is that a good thing or a bad thing?"

"What do you think?"

She shook her head. "Sarcasm does not become you, Sara. Sit down and calmly tell me what is bothering you."

I plopped into one of the wooden chairs circling

the round table. "Your guests are bothering me." I told her about Eleanor's failure as a babysitter and Henry appearing at Scoops in front of all my friends.

"Where is Henry now? And Buddy?" Her face wrinkled with concern.

"Buddy was with Mrs. Randazzo in their front yard when I walked home. She couldn't understand why I was hugging their dog so much when I saw him. Dad brought him back." I rested my hands on the brocade tablecloth. "I managed to get Henry upstairs into the closet. It wasn't easy. He loves that dog."

"So it seems. But everything ended well?"

"Because of me. Lily and Mason and David and who knows who else think I just ran off on them. It's all Eleanor's fault."

"I am sorry, Sara. I realize Eleanor and Dwight are quite trying to have around." She rested her hands in the lap of her ash-gray skirt. "But Sara, you made the choice to leave Henry out while you went with Lily. It wasn't a wise choice."

"I know, but since Eleanor and Dwight showed up, everything has been upside-down." I didn't want to say that it had started once she became famous and all the clients appeared.

She reached for my hands. "Be patient. I am doing my best to help them find what they are looking for and move on. I truly am." Worry clouded her eyes. She treated her clients' troubles as her own.

I sighed. My anger had faded. I couldn't stay mad at her. "Okay."

She continued to hold my hands. Her thumb circled my palm. "Something else weighs on your mind. Tell me about it," she urged.

And so I told her about all the strange things that had been happening. The caramel bottle moving. The skeletons falling for no reason. The milk bottle toppling. The drink spilling. The ball changing direction.

"I think spirits did it, but I don't understand why I couldn't see them. I can always see them." I hesitated. "At least, I thought I could."

She let go of my hands and shakily pushed herself to her feet. She wandered about the room, running her finger over glass shelves and side tables as if checking for dust. She always moved when she was deep in thought.

"There's another explanation," she said finally. "Telekinesis."

"What's that?"

"The ability to move objects with only the power of one's mind," she explained. She turned to me. "You were there when all these events occurred. Did you do anything to move the caramel sauce? Did you focus on the bottle? Think about moving it?"

"I . . . I don't think so," I said.

"Did you *want* these things to happen?"

"Maybe. Kind of." I thought back. "I didn't want the skeletons to fall, but I did want to help Mason get out of there. Now that I think about it, we were able to get out of there when we did *because* those skeletons fell. And I did want the green bear, so I wanted Mason to win, so I kind of wanted that last bottle to fall. But is wanting something the same as actually moving something?"

"If you want it enough. The mind is a very powerful tool." Lady Azura studied me carefully.

"Do you think I can do this telekinesis?"

"Before today, I would've said no. It's not a power that I have tracked along our family tree." Lady Azura kept a detailed chart of the women in our family going back centuries. Not every woman had powers. They often skipped generations. My own mother had had no powers. And all the women with powers didn't have the same powers. Some could communicate with the dead, some could read minds, some could predict the future, some had visions when they touched personal objects, and some could do all.

"Telekinesis is very, very rare," she added. "It seems unlikely to me that you caused those things to happen. I believe your original idea of an unseen spirit is more correct."

"But I could be developing it. I could have it a little, right?" I wasn't sure how I felt about adding another power to my menu . . . but this seemed like a really useful power to have!

"Maybe, but telekinesis requires great mental strength and lots of practice to control it."

"Wait!" I jumped from my seat. "Is it possible that someone could *learn* how to do it?"

Lady Azura let out her husky chuckle. "Sara, you and I know all too well that anything is possible."

"So could Lily have done it? Could she have taught

herself?" I knew Lily had been practicing moving objects with her mind. She'd been trying to tell me something earlier. Could this have been her big secret?

"I do not believe this is something Lily could have possibly taught herself. It would have to be a latent power that has come to the surface . . . but I have never sensed that Lily has any powers. Have you?"

I wasn't sure. I didn't think so . . . but then again, other than Lady Azura, I had never met anyone with powers. Would I somehow sense it? Was it possible my best friend had powers too?

Lady Azura didn't know the answer. She was a big believer in keeping an open mind and letting the truth reveal itself. "If it is a spirit, you will eventually see it. If it is Lily, you will see that, too. And if it is you, the window will soon open wider and you will be able to better see what you can do." She lifted a small, see-through crystal from a porcelain bowl on her glass shelves. "This is clear quartz. Add it to your necklace."

"What's it do?"

"It enhances psychic abilities. If you possess tele-kinesis, this crystal will bring your powers into clearer view." Her brown eyes glimmered. "How exciting that would be. The first of us to mentally move objects!"

The doorbell chimed. Lady Azura checked the slim gold watch on her wrist. "Ah, Mrs. Merberg is back. Maybe we will make progress today."

"I'm going to my bedroom," I announced. "What about Eleanor and Dwight?"

Lady Azura smiled. "They are mine now. The house will be quiet for a while."

Upstairs, I passed Dad straightening the room where we watched TV. He was muttering something about the house being a mess.

Tell me about it, I thought.

I closed my bedroom door. I sat straight on my chair with my feet on the floor and placed a yellow pencil flat on my desk. I needed to see what I could do.

I was going to move the pencil across the desk, I decided.

I stared at the pencil.

I focused on the pencil. Only the pencil.

My eyes crossed. The yellow blurred.

I tried to move the pencil.

A vein on the side of my head throbbed.

Nothing happened. The pencil stayed where it was.

I took a deep breath and tried again. Still nothing.

Maybe if I don't focus so hard, I thought. I stared at the pencil and thought about seagulls, waffles, and rain. Anything but the pencil moving.

It still didn't go anywhere.

I tried for twenty minutes, then gave up.

Lily had been with me when all those strange things happened, I realized. All of them, except the skeletons, but that could have been an opening-day mechanical failure.

It would be so cool if it were Lily moving things with her mind. Best friends, both with powers. Should I text her? Call her? How would I go about asking her?

I had no idea.

I stared at the pencil again.

One more time, I decided. I'd try to move it myself one more time.

Chapter 10

The whole next day I tried and tried. Pencils. A sneaker. My toothbrush. Even a cotton ball.

Nothing budged.

Perched on the high stool at the table in my crafts room that afternoon, I peered out the window. The sky was gray with misting rain. Fog blocked the view of the bay. Dad was at work. Lady Azura was with a client. Lily had gone with her family to visit a great-uncle.

The house was quiet.

I was arranging clamshells in a circle, overlapping one on the other to make a wreath, when I heard the first creak.

Creaks weren't a big deal. Our house always creaked. It was old. It had ghosts.

But the creaks grew louder.

They turned to scraping. And then to strange thumping.

I sat still and listened. The noises came from overhead. Something or someone was in the attic.

My fingers drummed the table as I watched the ceiling. *Boom. Thud.* What was going on up there?

Lady Azura couldn't help. She couldn't climb the stairs because of her bad hips.

I'd ignore it until Dad came home, I decided.

I busied myself arranging the wreath. A sudden sharp squeak of rusted hinges jolted my hand, knocking the shells out of place.

No way could I ignore it.

Slowly I made my way up the narrow staircase that led from the third floor into the attic. My heart fluttered as I reached the top stair. A tingling began in my left ankle.

It's probably just mice, I told myself. Or maybe a trapped squirrel. I prayed that was all it was. Even so, I wished I'd brought one of Dad's golf clubs or even my hot-glue gun.

Taking a deep breath, I peered into the attic's large open space, ready to run. Ready to scream.

Instead I just shook my head.

The two elderly spirits were rummaging through boxes of Christmas ornaments. They'd opened cedar chests. They'd knocked over old, unwanted furniture.

Eleanor and Dwight. At it again.

I turned to go, then stopped in horror. Eleanor had rested her plump hands on a large, upright wardrobe trunk. Her shimmery fingers fumbled with the brass clasps. She was opening the trunk.

My mother's trunk.

The trunk filled with her beautiful dresses.

The trunk filled with her smell.

The trunk that contained my small connection to her.

"No way!" I cried. I ran at Eleanor, leaping over a stack of vinyl record albums. "That's mine!"

Eleanor's tiny buttonlike eyes widened. She backed away.

I stood protectively in front of the trunk. They'd gone too far this time. "This doesn't belong to you!" I cried.

Dwight glanced up, then returned to rummaging through a canvas bag of old beach toys.

"None of this belongs to you," I said. "You can't

snoop through other people's stuff. What are you looking for?"

"We don't know. But we can't stop," Eleanor said pitifully. She turned to rifle through a pile of books. "We know it's here. Or somewhere."

"How will you know when you find it, if you don't know what you're looking for?" I was getting frustrated.

They both stopped. "We'll know. We will know because the anxiety will leave," Dwight said.

"Anxiety?" I asked.

"We both feel it. Like when you misplace your keys. Or forget your friend's birthday," Dwight explained. "We know what we're looking for, but we can't remember. We just know we need to find it."

This was growing more confusing by the minute.

"So you lost something? Maybe a key? Or a wallet? Was it a card in a wallet? Is it a photo?" I ran through a list of possibilities.

Dwight shook his head after each. Eleanor wrung her hands together.

I kept tossing out things they could've lost. Dwight stood by an old suitcase covered with travel stickers. He ran his hand over each one in a daze. His narrow shoulders slumped in distress. Eleanor wandered about. "Where? Where?" she muttered.

I tapped my foot restlessly. My eyes darted from a broken vacuum to a one-armed doll to the dusty stack of faded board games. I was overcome by a desire to open every box in the attic. I wanted to find it too. I didn't know what it was, but I wanted to find it to calm my now jittery nerves.

I bit my lip. The spirits' emotions were seeping into my body. I couldn't let that happen. Whenever it did, it caused trouble and I felt sick. I had to separate myself.

I bolted down the stairs, leaving Dwight still touching the travel stickers and Eleanor peering under a mousetrap. I ran all the way to the first floor.

I felt bad for Eleanor and Dwight. I finally understood their helplessness. Their yearning.

I pushed aside the purple curtain. The spicy scent of Lady Azura's cinnamon candles greeted me.

"The empress, the mighty one, has shown herself," Lady Azura was saying. She bent forward in her armchair, peering at the tarot card lying faceup on the table. A woman in a flowered dress, with red hair swooped into a bun, sat across from her.

They both stared at me.

"What is wrong?" Lady Azura asked, alarmed.

"Nothing, well, it's not an emergency," I fumbled. I wished I had thought before I barged in. Lady Azura hated to have her clients interrupted. "Something happened upstairs."

"Happened?" Lady Azura narrowed her eyes, trying to understand my meaning. "Did something *move* for you?"

"No. Not that. Eleanor and Dwight," I said.

She sighed. "Everyone is safe? Everyone is where they should be?"

"Yes. I just wanted to talk to you about helping them."

Lady Azura pursed her scarlet lips. "I am helping Ms. Moss now. There's lemonade in the fridge. We'll talk later, Sara." That was my hint to leave.

I stepped back into the foyer.

Eleanor and Dwight waited for me. Dwight carried an old flight bag. The leather had cracked, and the airline logo was flaking off. He must've found it in the attic.

Their bewilderment and frustration continued to flow into me. The strain of it tightened the tendons of my neck. They needed to be free of this burden they had carried with them into death.

I sat on the bottom stair. "She's busy," I whispered. "She's always busy. I wish I could help."

Then I wondered, could I? I had powers too.

Lady Azura always said that with training, my powers could be stronger than hers. I had been the one who found the Meyers' missing jewels. Lady Azura had kept my part out to protect me. To give me a normal life. To keep my secret.

But it was me.

If I'd helped them, why couldn't I help Dwight and Eleanor?

I listened to the low tones of Lady Azura's voice filtering through the curtain. Then I ushered Dwight and Eleanor onto the front porch.

For a moment I just stared at them. I had no idea what came next.

Okay, Sara, they're looking for something. You need to find what that something is, I told myself. It was like being a detective. I'd seen enough crime shows on TV. A detective searches for clues and hidden information. I could do that too.

"Hold on to me," I instructed Dwight and Eleanor.

I couldn't feel their hands as they gripped my arms. Closing my eyes, I tried to empty my mind. I needed to absorb more than just their emotions. I needed to absorb concrete thoughts. Secrets.

I concentrated.

Waited. Focused.

Then I heard a voice.

"Good afternoon, young lady."

Something was happening! I kept my eyes closed.

"Excuse me. Care to take this?" The voice was gruff.

My eyes flew open as I startled backward. Our mail-man in his blue postal uniform and dark sunglasses stood on our porch. He held a rolled-up magazine and some letters out to me. I was blocking the black metal box affixed to our house.

"Sure." I watched Eleanor and Dwight wander off to inspect a wheelbarrow Dad had left in the yard. Dwight still carried the flight bag. I didn't know why he liked it so much. He wasn't going anywhere.

Our mailman moved on to the next house.

I needed to find a way to help Eleanor and Dwight move on too.

Chapter 11

The milky-white gemstone caught the light from the window, shining like a full moon. I nestled the necklace in midnight-blue tissue paper, then covered the small box with silver star stickers. Lily would love my present when she opened it at the party tonight.

What would her wish be? I wondered.

If the moonstone was mine, I'd use it to give me courage. I was dying to find out what Lily could do and tell her what I could do. I'd almost called several times over the last two days. But fear kept me from dialing and kept that hard lump burning in my stomach. It was painful, but not as painful as losing Lily and all my friends. But if Lily's secret was the same as my secret . . .

"Sara? You up there? We're here!" Lily bellowed from the first floor. She had incredible lung power.

Buddy's barking carried up to my crafts room too.

Banging started from inside the closet. Henry had heard the barking. Why did Lily bring her dog? I wondered.

"Stop it," I hissed to the closet door. There was no way I was opening it.

"Come on, Sara!" Avery called up. "It's party time!"

Henry pounded the door with his small fists. Over and over. He wanted out.

I felt badly, but it was Lily's birthday. Henry would just have to deal. I ran downstairs to meet my friends.

Stopping just before I reached the foyer, I gaped in horror. Eleanor's shimmery hands pulled at Avery's shirt, as if she were trying to undress her.

Avery squirmed uncomfortably. She itched her neck. She adjusted her shirt. Then she adjusted it again.

Lily followed my gaze. "Aves, you got bedbugs or something?"

"Ew, don't say that." Avery scratched her collarbone. "It must be this shirt. It's new. Maybe there's something in the fabric."

"It's pretty," I said, forcing myself to sound calm.

I hurried down the last few steps. Avery's shirt was screen-printed with tiny airplanes in a rainbow of colors. I moved close to Eleanor. She was so busy running her ghostly fingers over Avery's shirt that she didn't see me.

It was bad enough to touch my stuff, but to touch my friends? No way.

I reached out as if to feel Avery's shirt and nudged Eleanor to the side. Eleanor seemed startled, as she stumbled away. "The fabric feels soft to me"—I made a point of actually touching the shirt—"but you can borrow one of mine."

Avery squirmed a bit more, then stopped and straightened her shirt. "It's kind of okay now."

Eleanor's arm reached toward her again. "Bob . . . Bob . . . Bob . . . ," she muttered.

I wedged myself between the babbling ghost and my friend. "Let's go celebrate, Lily!" I said.

"Let's go!" Lily agreed. "Buddy's walking to the boardwalk with us. Mom and Dad are already at Uncle Lenny's, setting up." That was the pizza place owned by her mom's brother. "My dad will take Buddy when we go to Midnight Manor."

Buddy barked when he heard his name.

"Sounds like a plan," I said, suddenly aware of the faint banging coming from upstairs. Henry longed for Buddy.

"You said you'd help." Eleanor's voice weighed low and heavy with sadness. Her arms fell limply to her sides. Even her helmet of white hair drooped, as if she were giving up.

I wanted to help them. But couldn't she see that I wasn't able to right now?

I followed Lily, Avery, and Buddy out the door and to the party, leaving Eleanor and Henry behind.

Lily was having a great time. We all were.

Uncle Lenny had decorated a large round table at the center of his restaurant. Tall with shiny black hair that swooped over his forehead, he presented pizza after pizza with a dramatic flourish. Each pizza had an L for Lily written on top—one with pepperoni, one with mushrooms, one with chicken. We sang "Happy Birthday" every time a new pizza arrived, which seemed to be every few minutes.

Miranda and Luke started a competition to see who

could eat the most red pepper flakes on their pizza without gagging. I was on Team Miranda.

My skin heated up as I watched her take a huge bite.

But the feverish feeling continued. Warmth pushed at my skin, crawling its way out from within my body.

I felt he was here even before I raised my eyes to the door. Mason met my gaze and held it for a half second. Did he feel it too? The heat, the static in the air, the connection?

He quickly looked away and loped over to Lily.

She beamed. "You came!"

"Happy birthday. Sorry I'm late." He shrugged apologetically. "My mom had to go somewhere first."

"Grab a chair," Lily said. "Sit anywhere."

Mason lifted a chair from a nearby table, scanned the twelve of us, then deliberately inserted himself between Avery and Luke. As far away from me as possible, I noticed. But why?

"So, who here has seen the movie *Mind Over Matter*?" Lily asked. Only half of us had, so Lily enthusiastically recounted the story of the movie, which had been a big hit about two years ago. In it, the main character has a lot of different paranormal abilities, including the ability to move objects with his mind. I knew from what I had learned from Lady Azura this meant the character had telekinesis, but I didn't offer that.

"Did you just see this or something?" Luke asked a little impatiently as Lily went into great detail about the movie plot.

Lily shot Luke a look that told him to be patient and continued with her story. "But at the end, the guy did the most amazing thing. He was sitting in a restaurant, just like this, and he placed a metal spoon in his hand. Without touching it, he made the spoon curl up. All of his friends were totally amazed."

"Curl up how?" Avery asked.

"Bend and curl into a circle," Lily explained.

"That's so not possible," Luke said.

"Yes, it is," Lily said. "The movie was based on actual events, so it really happened. Plus, I've been practicing mind bending at home. You need a lot of inner calm and positive energy."

Luke held up a spoon. "Okay, birthday girl, show us your stuff."

"It's not so easy. I've gotten close, but—"

"No excuses," Luke taunted. "Give it a bend."

Lily held the spoon in front of her nose. She stared intently at it. We all watched. Avery giggled, but Mason shushed her.

I licked my dry lips and waited, watching the spoon.

Could Lily do it?

The spoon stayed straight.

"Around the bend. Bend over backward. Bend it like—"

"Stop it, Luke," Lily said. "It's going to happen. I just need quiet."

Luke raised his hands in surrender. We all continued to watch Lily stare at the stiff spoon. Her expression grew serious. She was rarely serious. This meant a lot to her.

I focused on the spoon. I wanted it to bend.

I wanted it to bend for Lily.

I wanted it to bend so Lily and I would be the same.

I concentrated all my energy on the spoon. I could sense that Lily had relaxed her focus, so I increased mine. I really wanted it to bend.

Bend, I thought. *Bend*.

And then it did. The metal seemed to soften, and the bowl part of the spoon leaned to the left.

We all sucked in our breath. For a moment no one dared to speak. Then everyone exclaimed at once. Lily inspected the spoon, amazed at what she'd done.

Beads of sweat gathered along my hairline. My skin burned with a peculiar internal fire. I gazed at the spoon. Lily hadn't been the one to bend it. I was sure of that much.

Had I done it? I had been concentrating on it. I was pretty sure it had been me. I had done it.

I was the one with telekinesis.

Lady Azura would be so excited. I was the first in the family.

I felt his eyes on me.

Mason wasn't staring at the spoon like everyone else. He was staring at me. His piercing gaze traveled to the spoon, then back to me. He raised his pale eyebrows.

As if he knew.

Chapter 12

Our group marched together from Lenny's Pizzeria toward the red lights of Midnight Manor. Lily's mom led the way, and her dad and Buddy brought up the rear. Mason trailed behind me with some of the other boys. My skin tingled, knowing that he continued to stare at me.

What was he looking for?

Over our laughter and chatter, the Atlantic crashed along the beach. High tide had brought the ocean closer to the boardwalk tonight. The sun began to set, coloring the sky pink. Midnight Manor loomed before us.

I didn't want to go inside.

My mind churned with excuses. Just the thought of the horrors that waited made my skin crawl. But how could I disappoint Lily on her birthday? I was stuck.

"Hey, Sara, were you listening?" Avery gently tugged my purple patent wristlet with my money and phone. "Mrs. Randazzo is collecting all the presents and bringing them to Scoops, so we don't have to carry them through the haunted house. Lily's going to open them later when we go for ice cream."

"Oh no!" I stopped. "I left my present at home."

"That's okay. Give it to Lily tomorrow," Avery said.

"I really wanted to give it to her tonight. It's her birthday today, not tomorrow." What kind of best friend was I? I blamed Henry for pounding on the door and rattling me.

"I could come with you," Mason said over my shoulder.

"Come where?" I turned to face him.

"To get Lily's present. We could walk to your house now and meet up with everyone at Scoops."

"But you'd miss Midnight Manor," Avery pointed out.

Mason shrugged. "Opening presents is a big deal, isn't it?"

Why was he suddenly being nice? I'd never met a boy as confusing as Mason.

Then it hit me. He'd given me the perfect excuse to avoid the haunted house.

"I can go by myself." I didn't need Mason tagging along, staring and scowling at me. Or even worse, asking me how I'd bent that spoon. I went to find Mr. and Mrs. Randazzo.

They hated the idea. They refused to let me walk home by myself, even though it was only a couple of blocks.

Mason appeared by my side. "I can walk with her. My asthma gets really bad in there, anyway, because of the smoke machines."

"That's so nice of you," Mrs. Randazzo cooed.

He wasn't being nice, I realized. Mason was scared to go into Midnight Manor too. He'd pretended the other day that he wasn't, but I knew better.

It worked. With our promises to stay together, Mason and I were given permission to run back and get Lily's present. Mr. Randazzo handed Mason Buddy's leash. He asked us to walk the dog back to the Randazzos' house, where Lily's aunt was watching her brothers and sister. Lily's dad wanted to experience the "spookified" Midnight Manor.

All along the boardwalk, down Beach Drive and onto Ocean Grove Road, Mason and I only talked about the dog. We avoided everything else, especially the bending spoon. I'd never been so happy to have Buddy with me.

"I'll wait out here with Buddy," Mason said, when I stopped in front of our weathered yellow Victorian. The house had probably been grand a hundred years ago with its walk-out balconies, octagonal turret, and sweeping front porch. Now it just looked old.

"Out here? Why? Buddy can come inside."

"Just feel like it." His gaze landed on the sign. PSY-CHIC, HEALER, MYSTIC.

"Lady Azura won't mind." A car was parked by the curb. "She never comes out when she has a client. My dad's at a business dinner."

He hesitated.

"Look at Buddy. He's panting. He needs water. Come on." I grabbed Buddy's leash and led him up the front path, onto the porch, and into the house. Mason followed. We tiptoed past Lady Azura's purple curtain.

Mason dumped his black backpack onto the kitchen table as I filled a bowl at the sink. We both watched Buddy slurp the water. Neither of us knew what to say. In the small kitchen, I was aware of Mason standing close to me. The warm flush started in my palms. It snaked its way up my arms.

Why did I get this way? Could he tell?

I needed to say something to break the silence.

"What are those?" I pointed to a row of metallic pins lining the shoulder strap of his bag.

"My uncle, my mom's brother, is a pilot. He flies all over the world. He sends them to me. They're all from cool foreign airlines." He pointed to one. "This is from Air Tanzania. This one is from Royal Bhutan Airlines."

"That's neat," I said as Mason and Buddy climbed the stairs to the third floor with me. Dwight and Eleanor stood on the stairs, peering behind the framed coastal watercolors that hung on the stairwell walls. They moved aside for us, and I ignored them. "The farthest away I've ever been is California and Hawaii."

"Uncle Will once flew me to London," Mason said.

"What's London like?" I asked. We'd entered the crafts room. Mason described Piccadilly Circus and Big Ben. I heard the words, but I couldn't make sense of them. My body prickled with static. Every nerve stood at attention.

The walls of my craft room, always yellow, now glowed in brilliant rays. The swirly rainbow of my screen saver radiated, bursting from the monitor. Salt and decaying seaweed rose in a pungent wave from the collection of clamshells on the table.

What was going on? I'd never felt like this before. Did it have to do with spirits?

"Doggie!"

Henry's delighted cry ripped through my thoughts and jolted me out of my stupor.

I spun around.

The closet door stood open.

Henry's translucent body vibrated with joy as he spotted Buddy.

Mason peered into the closet. He held tight to Buddy's leash, keeping the dog just out of Henry's reach. "You've got a lot of art stuff."

"Nosy much?" I croaked, gaping at Henry.

Mason shrugged and walked to the window. Lights twinkled far out on the bay. "Those crabbing boats are late coming in," he remarked.

"Doggie!" Henry squealed again.

Buddy didn't seem to hear or sense Henry today. He didn't wag his tail. He stayed by Mason's side, loyal to his original boy. In a contest between Mason and Henry for Buddy's affection, Mason was the hands-down winner. And Henry did not like that.

He let out a cry of anguish. "Dog! Mine!" His eyes blazed, and he fixed a gaze of betrayal on Mason.

I needed to get Henry back in the closet. Fast!

Buddy rubbed up against Mason's leg. Mason leaned down and scratched his side as he continued to look out the window. Henry moved toward them. He glared at Mason as he reached for the dog.

Instinctively, I snatched Buddy's leash.

Mason whirled on me. "What are you doing?"

My skin burned with his gaze. "Let's decorate Buddy's collar. As a surprise for Lily," I quickly suggested. It was all I could think of. I led the dog toward the closet.

Henry followed. I knew he would.

"Now?" Mason crossed his arms. "Just grab the present. We're going to miss the ice cream, and that's the best part . . . even though you have such terrible taste in ice cream," he teased.

Why was he choosing now to suddenly act like the boy I'd been hoping for? Friendly. Nice.

"But I have an idea." I didn't really, but I'd come up with something, then shut Henry inside. I scanned the shelves.

Henry bent in the doorway and wrapped his arms around Buddy, burying his face into his fur. "Mine. Mine."

Mason stepped around me and into the closet. "Here. Tie this ribbon around him like he's a gift." He reached for a large spool of sheer red ribbon. It began to unravel on the floor.

"Whoa." I dropped Buddy's leash, as I fell to my knees to grab the falling ribbon.

The closet door slammed shut with a deafening bang.

"Hey!" I stood in complete darkness.

"What's going on?" Mason cried beside me.

Groping in the blackness, I heard scraping. Something heavy was being dragged across the floor. Then a *thump*, as it was pushed up against the other side of the door.

My hand found the smooth metal doorknob. It twisted, but the door wouldn't budge.

"I can't open it." I tried again.

"Let me." Mason's breathed on my neck. His arm brushed mine. It was like touching an electrical current.

I moved aside as his hand covered the knob. He pushed the door with his shoulder.

"Something's wedged against it." He grunted as he tried again. "How can that be?"

Buddy barked on the other side of the door. My throat tightened. We were locked in a tiny dark space. No one knew we were up here.

Henry had tricked us.

Chapter 13

I stood on my toes and grasped blindly. My fingers fluttered overhead.

Mason was so close to me.

The end of the cord tickled my fingertips. I yanked it, flooding the closet with light.

"That's better." Mason inspected the knob, then threw his side against the door. The door still didn't move. "This makes no sense. Buddy didn't do this."

"Where's your cell?" I asked.

"In my bag. In your kitchen." He groaned. "What about you?"

"In my bag. Also in the kitchen."

"We'll have to scream for your great-grandmother," he suggested, still pushing at the door.

"Lady Azura will never hear us. Her hearing is bad. Even if she did, she can't make it up all the stairs." I leaned my back against the shelves. "We're trapped."

"No, we're not!" He suddenly sounded frantic. He kicked at the door.

Buddy barked. He was still here. That meant Henry hadn't left.

"We've got to get out of here." Mason kept kicking. His frustration made the small space grow even smaller. The sleeve of his green T-shirt brushed my arm. His black sneaker stepped on my sandal.

"There's not enough room," he mumbled. The air grew stale and hot. His breathing grew faster as he pounded. "I hate small spaces." I saw beads of perspiration pop out on his forehead.

The supplies on the shelves rattled with his movements. Containers fell over. The air swirled with feathers, cotton balls, and dust.

"Just stop moving so much," I cried. My heart was hammering now.

"Why can't we get out?" he demanded. "What's going on?"

Buddy barked crazily on the other side.

Mason began wheezing.

"What's wrong? What's wrong?" I asked.

"Asthma," he managed. Desperately he struggled to fill his lungs.

I pushed aside a pile of feathers and pulled him to the floor. "You need to sit. Where's your inhaler?"

"Backpack." He kept wheezing. Short, ragged sounds. "There's no room in here."

He was panicking. Was this causing his asthma? "You have to relax."

Mason dropped his head into his hands. "Back away," he rasped.

I slid onto the ground and pulled my knees tightly to my chest, trying to take up the least amount of space possible. I was scared. What would happen if Mason didn't get his inhaler?

I have to get him out of here. He's not going to be okay without his inhaler. Sweat trickled down my neck. It was too warm in here. My skin crackled with a strange current. I needed to get out too.

"Henry!" I bellowed. "I know it was you! Let us out! Henry!"

Buddy barked.

"Henry!" I screamed again.

Mason lifted his head. "Who's . . . Henry?" Every

breath he sucked in sounded painful, but I was glad he could still talk.

Keep him talking. Keep him calm. I had no idea where the thoughts came from, but they were the only ideas I had.

"You're not going to believe it," I said quietly, leaning my head back, trying to open as much space as I could. I wanted to make him feel better. I wanted to reach out and hold his hand. Instead I just talked.

"Henry is a boy. A young boy. He's dead." I barreled forward, not waiting for Mason to respond. "He died back in the 1920s, I think. It's his spirit that's still here. Spirits do that sometimes. Get trapped. Henry lives in this house. Actually, he lives in this closet."

Mason said nothing, just wheezed. But his eyes were fixed on mine. He was listening.

"Henry was put in this closet because he's mischievous. He does pranks mostly. Makes messes and scares people. But before I came here, he found some matches and almost set the house on fire. Lady Azura couldn't control him, so she put him in the closet."

Mason's breathing was so labored I could barely look at him. I didn't want him to see the panic on my face. I stared at the brass doorknob. I kept talking. Calmly. Slowly. As if talking about ghosts was the most natural thing in the world.

"Henry went crazy for your dog when Lily brought him over last week," I continued. Was his breathing slowing now? Sounding less ragged? I talked more. There was a lot to tell about Henry. How he'd almost flattened Jayden with a bookcase at my Mischief Night party last fall. How he loved to make a mess in my craft room. When I was done telling stories about Henry, I realized that Mason's breathing was almost normal again. "He thinks Buddy belongs to him. He got upset when Buddy was so attached to you just now. That's why he put us in here. So he can be with Buddy. At least, I think that's why."

Mason nodded.

"I can see ghosts. Hear and talk to them too." The history of my seeing ghosts and coming to live with Lady Azura tumbled out. My brain couldn't keep up with my mouth. I told Mason everything.

"There are spirits everywhere. Most don't bother me, but others want help moving on. They're stuck here, because of unfinished business." I pointed to the door. "Not Henry, though. He's just here because he's having fun."

Mason didn't say anything. I realized I couldn't hear his breathing, which meant he was now breathing normally. And staring at me with the strangest look on his face.

"You must think I'm crazy," I said softly.

"No crazier than bending a spoon with your mind or toppling a milk bottle."

He'd seen that, too. How to begin to explain that? It was too new. Too confusing. We sat in silence for a very long time, listening to his wheezing.

"Do you believe me?" I asked.

"See that bottle of glue?" Mason pointed toward a white bottle on a shelf directly above our heads.

I nodded.

"Watch."

Slowly the plastic bottle inched its way along the edge of the shelf. It glided along, moved by unseen forces.

I turned to Mason. He was staring at the bottle. Really staring at it. Intensely staring at it.

"It's you!" I cried.

Chapter 14

Mason nodded. "I thought you knew. The way you act around me."

"Me? You're the one who's been acting weird," I said. "I didn't know it was you. Wow. So you can move whatever you want with your mind?"

He shrugged. "I guess. It's pretty crazy. Sometimes it just happens. I think my emotions trigger it. But if I focus on something, yeah, I can move it with my mind. "

My mind was still reeling. "Are you sure you bent that spoon? I thought maybe it was me."

"Really?" Mason scooted closer. "Try it. See if you can."

I focused on the glue bottle. Focused harder than I'd ever focused.

Mason watched me.

I watched the bottle.

It didn't move. At all.

"Yeah, you bent the spoon," I conceded. "Did you cause the skeletons to drop?"

"Yeah. I had to get out of there. The walls were closing in." He took several large gulps of air.

"You're not the only one, you know."

"Really?" He laughed. "Do you mean like the guy in the movie Lily was talking about? Would someone like us really want to have a movie made of our lives, showing off what we can do?"

Someone like us.

"No, I definitely wouldn't want to deal with all that attention . . . but the point is, there are other people out there like us. Lady Azura has powers too. You didn't know I could communicate with spirits, did you?"

"I knew something was up with you. That's why I tried to stay away."

"Up how? I thought you hated me."

Mason's checks flamed red. "I don't *hate* you. You just made me feel weird. Like there was this crazy electrical current zapping me every time you appeared." His green eyes searched mine.

"Me too. I felt it too. The connection."

He held my gaze for a long moment. Then we both squirmed uncomfortably.

"I need my inhaler." Mason stood abruptly.

"Can you unblock the door with your mind? I think Henry pushed my computer chair against it."

Mason's face took on that same faraway look I see in Lady Azura's eyes when she goes into a trance during a séance. He tried desperately to move the chair through the door. I stayed quiet and waited.

"It's not going to work," he admitted, wheezing slightly. "I can't focus on it without seeing it. Buddy stopped barking. Why's that?"

I pushed my ear against the door. I heard Buddy panting and then the repetitive thump of his wagging tail hitting the floor.

"Henry!" I shouted. "I know you're there with Buddy. Let us out!"

"You can still play with the dog," Mason called.

I smiled at him. "You just talked to a ghost."

"Yep. I figured you need all the help you can get."

"That's it!" I leaned against the door. "Eleanor! Dwight! Can you hear me?"

I continued to call their names. I knew they were close by. After a while, Dwight's limping shuffle brushed across the crafts room floor. Through the door, I instructed him to move the chair away. Unlike Henry, Dwight listened.

We burst out of the closet. Buddy bounded across the room and pounced on Mason. He covered his face with slobbery licks.

I glared at Henry as the little boy pouted.

Mason's eyes flicked about, searching for the dead people only I could see. "They're here?"

"Yeah."

"Cool." Mason stood. "I got to get my inhaler. We could leave Buddy up here for a little while if you want."

I followed Mason, Dwight, and Eleanor out, closing the crafts room door tightly. Henry would get a little more time with Buddy. I would deal with reprimanding him later.

Eleanor and Dwight dropped into chairs at the kitchen table. For once, they seemed tired from all their searching. Dwight still grasped that old flight bag.

I stood awkwardly by the refrigerator, watching Mason suck in air from his inhaler.

Had I really just told him everything? Everything I hadn't even told my best friend? It felt unreal. And embarrassing.

I watched him replace the inhaler in his backpack. I barely knew him. Up until a little while ago, I wasn't even sure I liked him. Could I trust him? Would he keep my secret?

Or had I just made a huge mistake?

Mason jiggled his leg and eyed me nervously. "I'm not going back to the party." He pulled out his phone. "I'm going to text my mom to come get me."

"Is your asthma still bad?"

"No. It's okay." He titled his head. "Thanks for mellowing me out up there. It helped."

"No problem. Why are you going home?"

"Not really in a party mood. Lots to process, you know?"

I did. "I probably missed the ice-cream part. I might as well text Lily and just meet up at her house for the sleepover."

"All-night party." His leg jiggled even faster. "What do you girls talk about for all those hours? Guys? Secrets?"

"Silly stuff." Then suddenly I knew why he was worried. "I won't say anything. About what happened. About what you can do. I promise. I'll never tell anyone."

He swept his hand through his spiky hair. "Same here. Just you and me. Our secret."

The warm tingle crept along my skin again. Our connection.

It felt good to have told someone.

The rock in my stomach had grown lighter.

"I was not expecting you home." Lady Azura entered the kitchen. Her arched brows raised when she saw Mason. "I certainly was not expecting you."

I explained about forgetting Lily's gift. Mason stiffened as Lady Azura looked him over. Could she sense his powers? I wasn't sure. She was definitely looking at him closely. But then again, it wasn't that often that she walked out into our kitchen and saw me sitting there with a boy. Well, I wasn't going to tell her. I'd made a promise.

"Got to fly. My mom's out front." Mason went to lift his backpack. Eleanor's pudgy hands were playing with the pins. She grabbed on. Panic seized her shimmery body. I felt her panic.

"Bob?" she whispered.

Mason didn't hear her, didn't feel her pull. He yanked the bag up onto his shoulder and left through the back door.

Lady Azura headed to the pantry to make her nightly hot chocolate. I'd been the only one to hear Eleanor. My mind sorted through all the bits and pieces. The flight bag. Avery's shirt. The pins.

"Is there someone in Eleanor and Dwight's life who's a pilot?" I asked suddenly. "Someone important?"

"Yes. They had a son who was a pilot."

"Was?"

Lady Azura turned. "He died."

"How?"

"I do not know."

"Can you find out?" I asked.

"Yes. I'll ask Mrs. Merberg tomorrow. She mentioned him once. His name was—"

"Bob," I finished. "His name was Bob."

Lady Azura leaned toward me. "How did you know that?"

"I figured out who Eleanor and Dwight are searching for. They're searching for Bob."

147

Chapter 15

Even though it was late, Lady Azura went to call Mrs. Merberg.

"Bob was a pilot for the army," she reported when she returned. "Mrs. Merberg said that Bob—he was her cousin—was on a training flight out over the Pacific Ocean when his plane went down. The army never recovered his body."

"So he's dead? Buried at sea?" I asked.

"Most likely. But his parents always held out hope that he had swum to safety."

"Is that possible?"

"Doubtful. The military officially declared him dead." Lady Azura sat beside me at the table. Eleanor and Dwight had long since wandered off to some other corner of the house.

"Then what happened?"

"Eleanor and Dwight refused to have a funeral or a memorial for him. The idea upset them so much that they wouldn't speak of him or have anyone else speak of him. No one has mentioned Bob for over twenty years. It was as if he never existed."

"And now, to them, he never did. They forgot about him."

"Not completely. They're still searching for him. I suspect they fear crossing over and leaving their son behind, though they don't realize it. His unknown fate is what binds them here." Lady Azura folded her hands. "They need to reconnect with him, so they can all move on together."

"How does that happen?"

"I will perform a séance to bring Bob's spirit back. In death, he can reunite with his parents. Then they can all go on together to the same place." Lady Azura exhaled. "It will take a lot of work. A great deal of psychic energy."

"Mrs. Merberg will be happy you solved her problem. She'll write about you in her book."

"It was you who solved it, Sara. You." Lady Azura clasped my hands tightly between hers. "We will finish this together, if you'd like. Perform the séance together. Bring Eleanor and Dwight their relief together."

"Really?" I smiled. "I'd like that."

"Good." She leaned back. "I have been working too hard. It is not good for me, and it is not good for you."

"I'm fine—"

"Rubbish. You have not been happy. I closed my eyes to what was in front of me to look beyond. I was focused on the tops of the trees and ignored the roots. You moved here for my help, and I have been helping others instead."

"Lots of people need you," I said. I was proud of her. She was much more patient than I could ever be. I'd have sent Eleanor and Dwight packing and never would have discovered how to help them.

"I am taking a vacation. I am closing the business for a month. How does that sound?"

"It sounds great."

"Hot chocolate?" she asked. "With lots of marsh-mallows?" She held up the package.

"I can't miss any more of Lily's party," I said. As it was, I had a lot of explaining to do.

"I'll hold these then. A special treat." She replaced

the marshmallow package in the pantry and waved me away. "Go celebrate. Dwight, Eleanor, and I will see you tomorrow. And tomorrow we will talk more about that boy."

I felt my cheeks burn at her mention of Mason. "It's a deal," I promised.

I ran upstairs. I had to separate Henry from Buddy. First I did a little decorating. I plastered the closet walls with photos of Buddy. "He'll be with you always," I told Henry. Then I shut him away, grabbed the dog and Lily's present, and ran down the street.

Avery, Miranda, Tamara, and Marlee were already arranging their sleeping bags in Lily's family room by the time I flopped onto the sofa.

"So what's the deal with you and Mason?" Avery asked as soon as I hit the couch cushion.

"Yeah, Sar, what's the deal?" Miranda demanded. "I thought you guys didn't even like each other . . . but the way he went back to your house with you like that . . ." She waggled her eyebrows at me, à la Lily's favorite expression.

"He was being nice. We're just friends." *Or at least, we're finally starting to be,* I thought.

"You guys aren't a perfect match, after all," Lily admitted. "He's so up and down. Kind of moody."

"My big sister had this one boyfriend, and he liked her and then he didn't and then he did again," Marlee added. "Mind games is what she called it."

I fought to hold back my grin. Mason definitely played mind games. But so did I.

I kind of liked that we shared that. Mind games.

"Enough boy talk for now!" I said, wanting to change the subject. "Open my present, Lil!"

Lily squealed and opened her present. "It's gorgeous!" she breathed as soon as she saw what was inside the box. She unwrapped the necklace, showing everyone. "Is this a crystal from Lady Azura's collection? Does it have powers? What does it do?"

"It's a moonstone. If you wear it close against your skin, it helps your most precious wish come true."

Lily squealed again and fastened the cord around her neck. "It's perfect. I absolutely love it!"

"What're you going to wish?" I asked. I already knew the answer. She wanted to do what Mason could do.

"I'm not sure. Until tonight, I thought my wish was to be able to move things with my mind. But I've thought more about it, and I'm not sure that's the coolest power."

"So have you made up your mind what power would be the best one?" Avery prompted.

Lily nodded and grinned. She looked right at me and her smile grew wider. "I bet you can guess, Sara. . . ."

"Me?" I croaked. "How could I guess?" My head was spinning. What was Lily going to say? Was she going to say she knew about my powers? I knew I had to talk to her about it very soon . . . but not now. Not in front of everyone else.

"Oh come on, Sara! Think about it!" Lily pressed. "You know, right?"

"No, not a clue," I croaked.

"How to talk to the dead," Lily said finally. "Lady Azura and I can do it together. Wouldn't that be so cool, Sara? Talking to the dead with Lady Azura?" Lily pressed the moonstone against her chest. "That's my wish. This stone will help me be able to do that. I just know it will work. This is the best birthday present ever!"

Could the moonstone really have that kind of power? I leaned back on the sofa cushion and cringed. What kind of present had I just given her?

From now on, I was only handing out gift cards.

Want to know what
happens to Sara next?

Here's a sneak peek at the next book in the series:

Playing with
Fire

The front door swung open, taking me by surprise. I sucked in my breath, startled to see him.

To see him with Lily.

I'd just jogged up the Randazzos' walkway. I hadn't yet reached out my hand to ring the bell, and there he was.

His green eyes sparkled with recognition. I did everything to keep my lips from curling in a smile. We held a secretive gaze for a moment, before I looked away.

After all this time, it was strange to see him in front of me. No longer just words illuminated on a tiny screen.

"Sara!" Lily cried. She hadn't been expecting me, but it was a hot day in August and I was bored. It was the kind of day meant for showing up at your best friend's door "This is great. Mason's here."

"Hey there," I said softly as I shifted my weight uncomfortably.

"Mason's hanging out with Buddy," Lily continued. Her little brown dog panted beside Mason's ankle. Buddy had been Mason's dog but his mom was allergic, so Lily's family had taken Buddy in. "His mom dropped him off while she went to the doctor."

Dr. Shiffer, I wanted to say. He specializes in migraines. Mrs. Meyer has been getting super-bad headaches lately, and Mason has to watch his brother and sister. Mason's mom heard about Dr. Shiffer from a friend and is hoping he will be able to help her.

But I couldn't say that.

I couldn't say that and not say a whole lot more.

"Sara and I've spent the whole summer on the beach," Lily told Mason, not knowing that Mason already knew that. That Mason knew pretty much everything that was going on with me. She pointed to the black Nikon camera I wore around my neck. "She's been doing this thing where she takes a photo of the same spot on the boardwalk every day at three thirty. Same background but always different people doing different things."

"Really?" Mason actually sounded surprised. As if he knew nothing about my hobby. As if he didn't call me "Eye Spy" in our texts. "What are you doing with them?"

"She's been printing out the photos," Lily answered. "She's going to mount them on a large board—"

"Actually, I'm thinking of binding them together and making a kind of flip book," I interjected. I fixed my gaze on my orange sandals. I couldn't look at Mason. The flip book had been his idea yesterday.

"Oh, I love it!" Lily's maple-syrup-brown eyes widened. "You could sell that at one of Stellamar's souvenir shops, you know. Print a lot of them. Mason, isn't that totally original?"

"Totally." Mason smirked. "One-of-a-kind. I can't believe *you* thought of that, Sara."

He thought he was being funny, but he wasn't. I smiled my biggest smile back at him, playing along. I was confident he wouldn't dare spill our secret. He knew Lily could never know about us.

If she knew, she'd ask questions.

Questions neither of us wanted to answer.

My stomach twisted. I felt bad. Lily Randazzo was

my best friend. She'd be humiliated if she knew Mason and I were playing at barely knowing each other.

I also knew what Lily would think if she found out that we'd been texting almost every day for the last month. She'd think we liked each other. She'd think we were together.

But we aren't.

We're just friends. I scratched my shoulder and flinched as bits of post-sunburn skin flaked off. There was no way Lily or any of our other friends would believe me. I didn't text with any other boys. Plus, Mason wasn't even from our school. He lived almost thirty minutes away. And he was cute. Really cute. White-blond hair. Tanned skin. Wide-set eyes.

If I didn't like him, she'd want to know what I was doing. Why I was talking all the time to a supercute guy. Guys and girls our age usually don't talk all the time unless they like each other. What could we possibly be talking about? she'd want to know.

And the answer to that question was complicated.